Praise for my ... ks

'Will make you laugh out loud, cringe and snigger, all at the same time'
-LoveReading4Kids

... funny and cheeky'
-Booktictac, Guardian Online Review

Waterstones Children's Book Prize Shortlistee!

'I LAUGHED SO MUCH, I THOUGHT THAT I WAS GOING TO BURST!'
Finbar, aged 9

'The review of the eight year old boy in our house... "Can I keep it to give to a friend?" Best recommendation you can get' -Observer

'HUGELY ENJOYABLE, SURREAL CHAOS'
-Guardian

I am still not a Loser
WINNER of
The Roald Dahl
FUNNY PRIZE
2013

First published in Great Britain 2014
This edition published in 2016
by Jelly Pie, an imprint of Egmont UK Ltd
The Yellow Building, 1 Nicholas Road, London W11 4AN

Set ISBN 978 0 6035 7165 7
Book ISBN 978 1 4052 6802 8

barryloser.com
www.jellypiecentral.co.uk
www.egmont.co.uk

A CIP catalogue record for this title is available from the British Library

Printed in Great Britain by the CPI Group

60285/2

Barry Loser

and the holiday of doom

Colour of cover decided by

Jim Smith

Frilly pink bikini

My best friend Bunky is sort of like my pet dog, so it was weird when he suddenly started fancying a cat one day.

It was about eight million weeks ago and me and Bunky were walking home from school past a Feeko's Supermarket.

Summer was coming up, and the whole window was filled with swimming trunks and other holidayish things like that.

'You should buy those for Sharonella!' giggled Bunky, pointing at a bunch of fake plastic sunflowers.

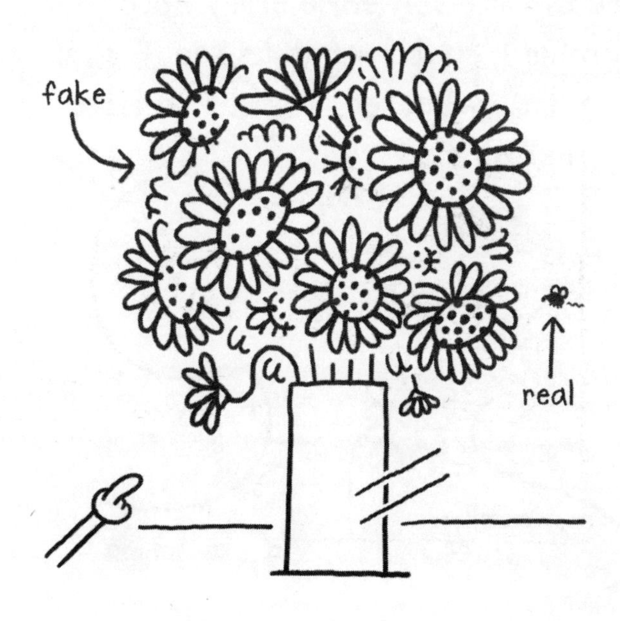

Bunky's been saying Sharonella from our class fancies me ever since she said I had a nice nose once.

'Shut up, Bunky!' I said, looking down at my nose and trying to work out what was so good about it. 'How can someone like someone else's nose?' I mumbled, twitching it to see if that made it any better. 'It's just a nose for smelling stuff with.'

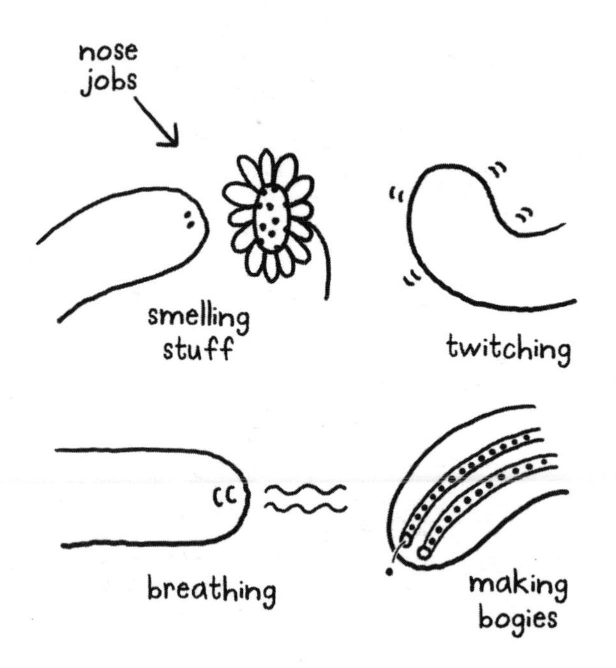

I tried to think of someone who fancied Bunky's nose, but all I could come up with was my other best friend Nancy Verkenwerken, who's sort of like my pet cat.

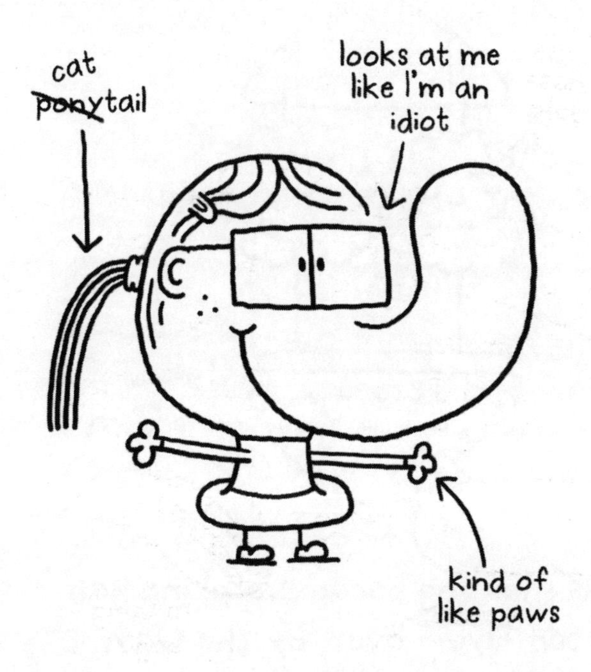

'YOU SHOULD BUY THAT FOR NANCY!' I shouted, pointing at a pink frilly bikini.

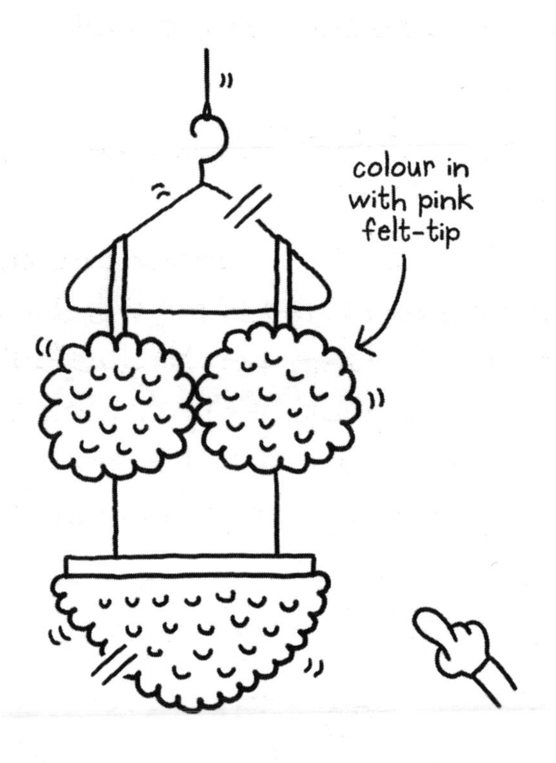

I was shouting because a plane had started flying over, by the way.

Bunky's whole face turned the same colour as the bikini, but less frilly. 'I DON'T FANCY NANCY!' he shouted, fiddling with a bit of old bubblegum someone had stuck on the wall.

I looked at Bunky. Something about the way he'd said it made me wonder if he actually DID fancy her. He'd definitely been smiling a lot at Nancy recently, but then Bunky smiles at everyone. That's what sort-of pet dogs do.

And that's when I noticed something. The whole time we'd been standing there, Bunky had been busy squidging the bubblegum into the shape of a heart.

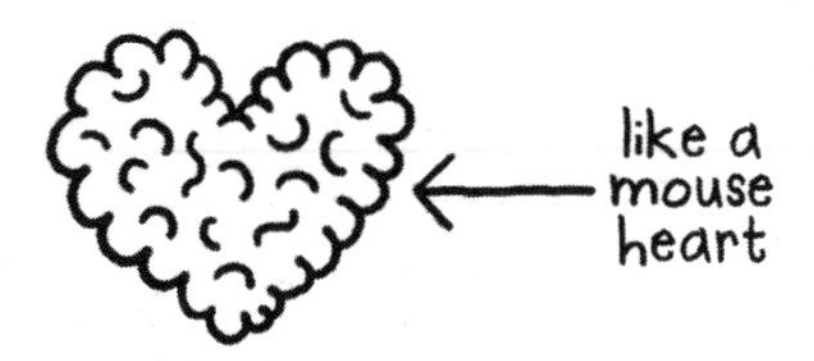

'WHAT IN THE NAME OF UNKEELNESS?!' I gasped, which is what my favourite TV star **Future Ratboy** says when he can't believe his eyes.

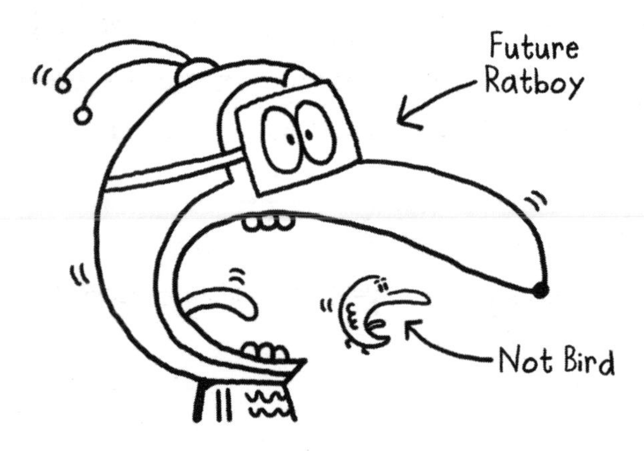

'Huh?' said Bunky, gazing through the window at a pair of sunglasses the same shape as Nancy's specs.

I looked at my half-dog, half-best-friend and imagined him bounding through a field of fake plastic sunflowers, his dog lead being held by Nancy Verkenwerken instead of me. All of a sudden I felt a bit queasy.

'I'M GOING TO BE SICK,' I shouted, even though the plane had completely flown off.

Plonkton

When I got home my mum and dad were standing in the kitchen, smiling like it was Christmas morning.

'What is it?' I said, hoping they'd finally bought me a puppy. I'd been asking for a real-life pet dog for nine trillion years now, and I STILL didn't have one.

'Barry, you know how we're going on our caravan holiday to Plonkton this weekend?' said my mum.

She had a tea towel on her shoulder, and my dad was standing right behind her, leaning his head on it like a cabbage.

'Ye-ah?' I said, splitting my yeah into two bits because of how keel Plonkton is.

'Well your mum and me were thinking maybe you'd like to invite a couple of your little pals along?' said my dad's cabbage head.

The words swam down my earholes and into my legs, making them go wobbly.

I leaned against the washing machine, which had been busy washing our best clothes for Plonkton all week.

'What, like Bunky and Nancy?' I said all shakily, probably because the washing machine was wobbling around like some kind of giant metal jelly cube.

'Yes, like Bunky and Nancy!' chuckled my mum, and I gave her a cuddle, imagining how disgusting it'd be if she was Sharonella from my class.

I picked up the phone to tell Bunky and Nancy, then changed my mind, deciding it'd be keeler to see their excited little dog and cat faces face-to-face.

After that I played nineteen games of **Future Ratboy** on my Feeko's Gamoid to celebrate.

Then I brushed my teeth with my **Future Ratboy** toothbrush, got into my **Future Ratboy** pyjamas and snuggled up underneath my **Future Ratboy** duvet to go to sleep.

'Wait till Bunky and Nancy hear!' I whispered to my cuddly **Future Ratboy**, and I squeezed his fat little belly and waited for him to speak.

'WHAT IN THE NAME OF UNKEELNESS?!' he screeched, and I remembered me saying the exact same words to Bunky outside Feeko's that afternoon.

'What if Bunky DOES fancy Nancy?' I yawned, and I squeezed his belly again.

'PUKESVILLE-O-RAMA!' he screeched, as I nodded off to sleepypoos.

Kangaroo jacket

It was the next morning and I was sitting on my own in our classroom at school. I usually meet Bunky at the end of my road and skateboard to school with him, but for some reason today I'd com-per-lee-ter-ly missed him.

'Morning, Barold!' said Darren Darrenofski, wobbling through the door slurping on a can of Fronkle. He took his jacket off and hung it on my nose.

'Be a loser and look after that,' he burped, just as I spotted a sticker of a kangaroo doing a thumbs up stuck on to his jumper.

Our teacher, Miss Spivak, had started giving out scratch-and-sniff stickers to people for being well behaved, and even though I'd been a good little Barry for about nine trillion days in a row, I still didn't have one.

'How in the name of loserness did you get that?' I said, because Darren's the baddest-behaved person in the whole class.

'I peeled it off Gordon Smugly's jumper when he wasn't looking!' grinned Darren, giving the sticker a scratch, and I breathed in through my nostrils to see if it really did smell of kangaroo, not that I could smell anything apart from the inside of Darren's jacket, which actually did stink a bit like a kangaroo I'd smelled at Mogden Zoo once.

'That's not fair!' I said, standing up and waggling my nose, and Darren's jacket flew off my nose into Miss Spivak's bin.

'Ooh, what a luvverly strong nose you have, Bazza!' said an annoying voice, and I spotted Sharonella sitting down at the table next to me, stinking of perfume.

All of a non-sudden Miss Spivak walked into the classroom with Honk the class parrot on her shoulder. 'I saw that,' she squawked. 'I'm watching you, Loser.'

'But . . .' I said, starting to explain how it was all Darren's fault for hanging his kangaroo jacket on my nose, but Miss Spivak wasn't listening.

'I'll never get a scratch-and-sniff sticker now!' I whisper-shouted to Darren, and Sharonella reached over and scratched my earlobe.

'You smell nice enough already, Bazza!' she smiled, sniffing her finger, and I was just about to tell her how much she stank, when Bunky and Nancy walked through the door.

Something wrong with Bunky

'Mornkeels!' I said, grinning at them. I was so excited to tell them they were coming to Plonkton, I wasn't even annoyed that they'd walked to school together instead of with me.

'Hi Barry,' said Bunky, smiling at Nancy, who was wearing a scratch-and-sniff sticker of a mushroom doing a thumbs up she'd got for being the best at spelling.

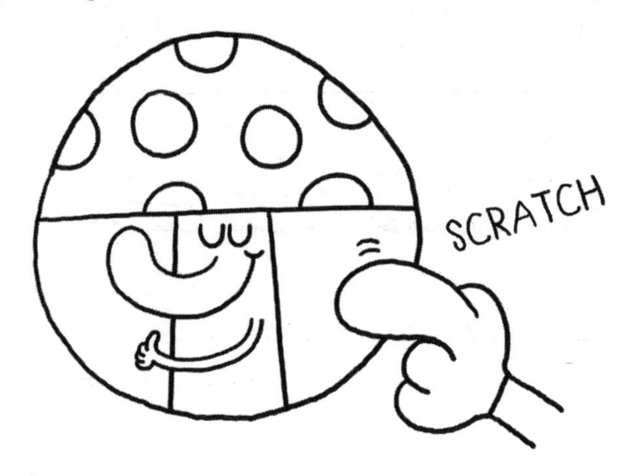

I looked at my half-dog, half-best-friend and wrinkled my forehead. There was something about him that didn't make sense.

I Future-Ratboy-zoomed my eyes in and tried to work out what it was.

His trainers looked normal, all scuffed up and stinking of foot cheese like they always did.

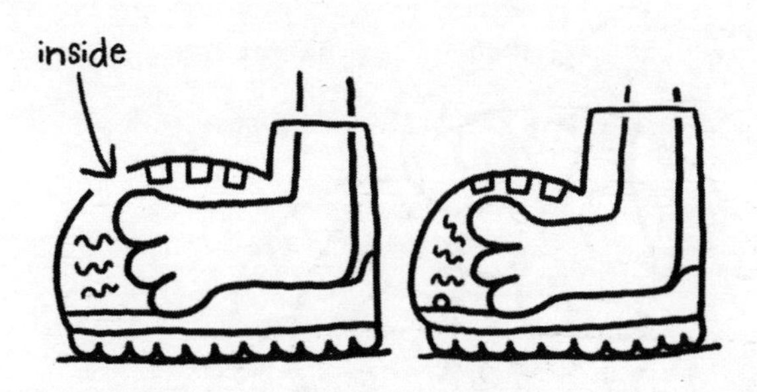

His legs were just his boring old legs, standing there with the rest of him balancing on top of them.

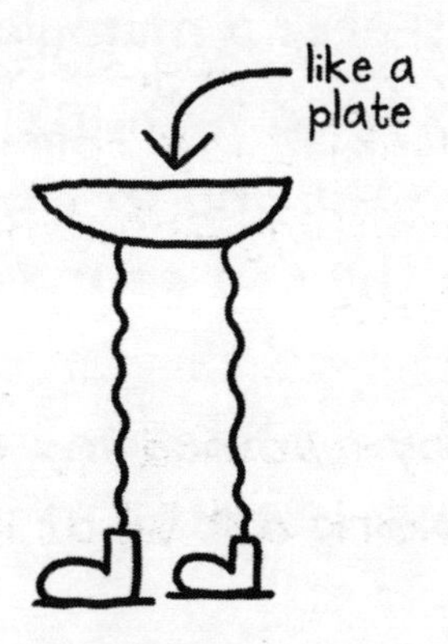

And his nose, ears, eyes and mouth were dotted around on his head in pretty much the right places.

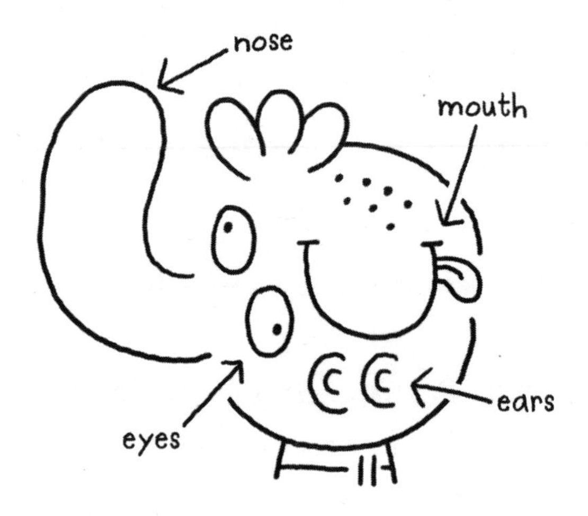

'What else is there?' I mumbled, scratching my head with my fingers, which were on the end of my hand, which was on the end of my arm.

And that's when it hit me.
Bunky was holding a BOOK.

Goody-goody Bunky

'W-what is THAT?' I stuttered.

The whole time I'd known Bunky I'd never seen him even look at a book, and now he was carrying a PINK one with a picture of a KITTEN on it.

'Weird, isn't it!' chuckled Nancy, prodding Bunky like she was checking to see if he was real. 'It's not HIS, of course.' She slid the book out from under Bunky's arm and put it down on her desk.

'He said he wanted to carry it for me. I honestly don't know what's got into him recently!' she smiled.

'Nothing's got into me, I'm just being well behaved so I get a sticker!' said Bunky, scratching Nancy's mushroom one and sniffing his finger. He grinned at Nancy, and his eyes scrinched up into two little upside-down grins as well.

I was just about to tell him to wipe all three of his loserish grins off his face, when Miss Spivak started calling out the register.

I always get nervous waiting to hear my name being called out, and in the panic I forgot all about Bunky carrying the book.

'I'M HE-ERE!' I shouted when Miss Spivak finally said my name, and I breathed a sigh of relief.

To celebrate it being over, I thought I'd tell Bunky and Nancy the good news about Plonkton.

'Psst, Bunky! I've got the keelest news ever!' I whispered-shouted into his ear, and I waited for him to say, 'WHAT IS IT?' all excitedly, his nose wagging like a dog's tail.

'LOSER!' shouted Miss Spivak, putting her finger up to her lips. 'Don't make me lose my rag!'

'Oh yeah, sorry!' I whispered, remembering how we were all supposed to be being good boys and girls, what with the scratch-and-sniff stickers and everything.

I squeezed my lips together as tightly as possible and crossed my arms, trying to be the best little Barry I could.

I really really wanted a scratch-and-sniff sticker, and it's not like I couldn't wait till break to tell Bunky and Nancy they were coming to Plonkton.

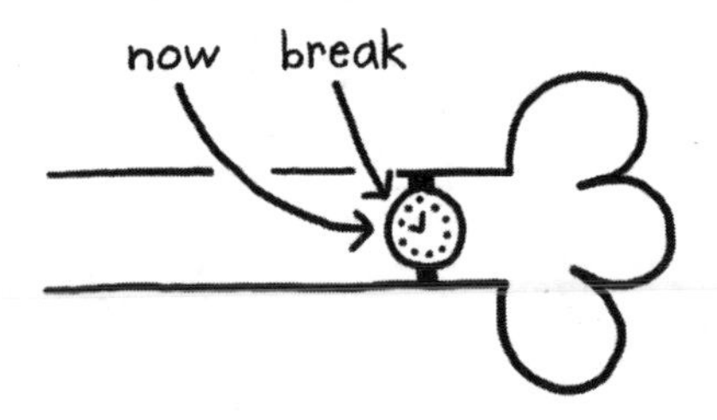

Except I comperleeterly couldn't.

Bad doggy

'Psst, Bunky! My mum and dad said you and Nancy could come to our caravan in Plonkton this weekend!' I blurted as fast as possible so Miss Spivak wouldn't hear.

Bunky turned his head round all slowly, so Miss Spivak wouldn't see. 'Shhh!' he whispered, then he smiled at Nancy, who was too busy reading her kitten book to take any notice.

'But . . .' I whispered, and my but floated round the classroom like a butterfly chopped in half.

I knew Bunky wanted a scratch-and-sniff sticker, but this was ridiculoserous.

'Did you hear what I just said?' I said, which is what I say when I can't believe someone hasn't heard what I've just said.

'I heard you loud and clear, Bazza!' whisper-squawked an annoying noise from the table next to me. I swivelled my eyeballs to the left and saw Sharonella batting her eyelids at me.

'You can take me to Plonkton any time!' she grinned, looking at my nose, which was sticking out of my face, trying not to smell her perfume.

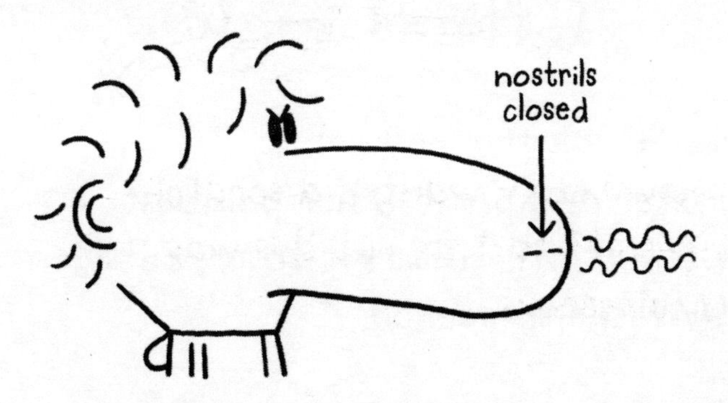

'IT'S JUST A NORMAL NOSE!' I shouted, an excitement blowoff from earlier popping out as an extra-loud annoyance fart, and I turned back to Bunky. 'HELLO-O?' I boomed, knocking on his head like it was a front door. 'ANY-BODY HO-OME?'

Miss Spivak stopped calling out the register and pointed her pointiest finger at me. 'That's it Loser, outside NOW!' she screeched.

I stood up and looked at Bunky sitting there all goody-goodily, trying to impress Nancy.

'BAD DOGGY!' I said, wagging my finger at him, and I stormed out of the classroom.

Smelly light switch

I was in the corridor, scratching-and-sniffing a light switch, when the bell went and the door swung open and everybody started running out.

'Thanks a LOT for getting me in trouble!' I said, smelling Bunky's cheesy feet standing behind me. 'I'm never gonna get a scratch-and-sniff sticker now,' I moaned, turning round and doing a surprise blowoff.

It wasn't Bunky, it was Darren Darrenofski, wearing a brand-new sticker with a triangle of cheese doing a thumbs up on it.

'How in the name of loserness did you get that?' I said, snuffling my nostrils all around it like a dog.

'I peeled it off Anton Mildew's jumper when he wasn't looking!' burped Darren, the smell of his Fronkle burp mixing in with the cheese sticker and Gordon's kangaroo one from earlier.

As if there weren't enough bad smells already, Sharonella floated up. 'Poor old Anton. You're a bad boy, Dazzer!' she chuckled, high fiving Darren, and the noise of their palms slapping together made me blink.

When I opened my eyes again twelve billiseconds later, Bunky was walking out of the classroom behind Nancy Verkenwerken.

I turned round to tell him off for getting me in trouble and gasped.

Stuck on to his jumper was a scratch-and-sniff sticker of a Diplodocus doing a thumbs up.

Plankton

'WHAT IN THE NAME OF UNKEELNESS?!' I shouted, even though there wasn't a plane flying over.

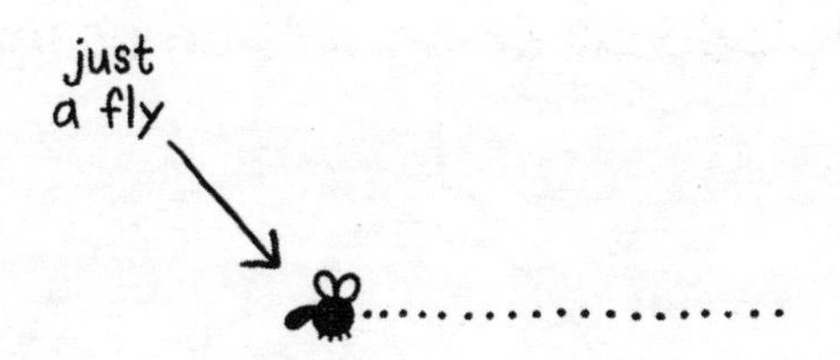

'Miss Spivak gave it to him for being a good little doggy!' cackled Darren, and Sharonella giggled.

I looked at Bunky, standing next to Nancy like he was her dog instead of mine, and comperleeterly lost my rag.

'What HAS got into you, Bunky?' I shouted, sounding exackerly like my mum.

Bunky looked down at me and smiled, but not the way he would have if I'd been Nancy.

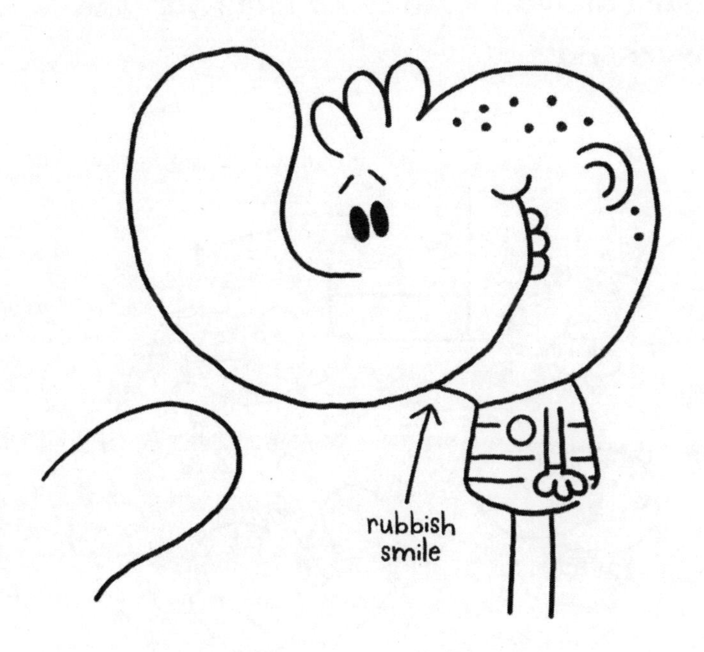

'Oh yeah, sorry about in there, Barry,' he said. 'What were you saying about Plankton?'

'Plonkton! It's Plonkton!' I shouted, my voice bouncing off his belly because of how short I am. 'My mum and dad said you and Nancy could come on our caravan holiday to Plonkton this weekend!'

Bunky looked at Nancy, then at me, like a dog trying to decide which one of us was its real owner.

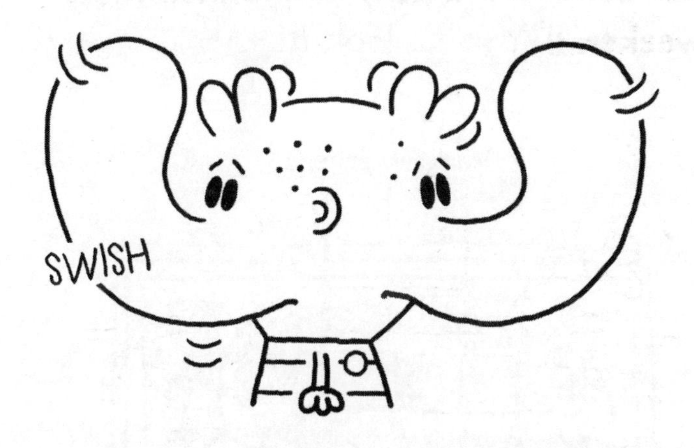

'Thing is . . .' he said, fiddling with a drawing pin sticking out of the wall.

I peered into his face, which he was wrinkling up like a piece of bubblegum, and wished I'd told him about Plonkton over the phone after all.

'You see . . . me and Nancy and her mum and dad and baby brother Keith were sort of gonna go and buy a kitten this weekend . . .' he said, scratching his Diplodocus sticker so he didn't have to look at me.

The words swam down my earholes into my legs, making them go wobbly.

'Wait a millisecond, let me get this straight,' I said, sounding like the detective in my mum's favourite TV show. 'You were gonna buy a kitten without telling ME . . . and now you're saying NO to the holiday of a lifetime?!'

I couldn't believe my ears, eyes, nose, legs and arms all put together.

'It's not like that, Barry,' said Nancy. 'We would've invited you, but we knew you were going to Plonkton . . .'

'Yeah, and we didn't know you were gonna invite us!' said Bunky, looking all confused.

My legs gave way from all their wobbling, and I reached an arm out for somebody to catch me. 'H-help me, I think I'm going to faint . . .' I gurgled, and Sharonella ran forwards and caught me in her arms.

'I'll go to Plonkton with you, Bazza,' she whispered in my ear, and it tickled, but not in a funny way.

I lay in Sharonella's arms, working out if I should take her to Plonkton, just to teach Bunky and Nancy a lesson.

And then I heard a voice.

'I suppose we could always get the kitten another weekend,' said Nancy, and I held my breath.

'You mean you'll come to Plonkton?' I gasped, even though I was supposed to be holding my breath, and my sort-of pet dog and cat both nodded their heads.

Cat Ears

'I'm so glad you changed your minds!' I beamed, walking home from school with Bunky and Nancy on Friday afternoon. I was in the best mood ever, even though I still didn't have a scratch-and-sniff sticker.

'It's gonna be the keelest!' barked Bunky. I fished around in my pocket for an old Thumb Sweet I'd been saving and threw it into his mouth.

'Thumb Sweets are my favourite!' he spluttered, bits of chewed-up thumb splattering all over the pavement.

Nancy smiled, swishing her ponytail like it was a cat tail. 'Tell us more about Plonkton, Barry!' she said, even though I'd been going on about it all week.

'Oh my keelness, where do I startypoos!' I said, doing a quadruple-reverse-upside-down salute with both hands, which is what I do when somewhere is as keel as Plonkton is.

'There's this amazekeel place called Gino's Pizza that does the tastiest pizza in the whole wide world amen,' I said. 'I'll introduce you to Gino. He's the person who owns it.'

Nancy glanced at herself in the reflection of the Feeko's we were walking past and chuckled. 'A place called Gino's Pizza owned by a person called Gino? What will they think of next?!' she smiled.

'Gino is the keelest! He sells these tiny little slices of pizza the exact same size as cat ears!' I said, pointing at Nancy's head, right where her ears would go if she was a real-life cat.

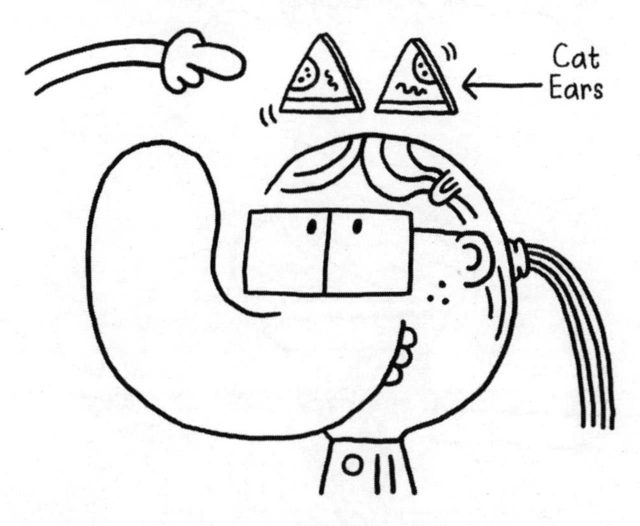

'Let me guess what he calls them . . . Cat Ears?' said Nancy, and I nodded, spotting that bit of bubblegum Bunky had squidged into a heart, still stuck on the wall.

'What does he call his chocolate ice cream? Dog Poo?' laughed Bunky, and I sniggled through my nose, wondering if this was the happiest I'd ever been in the history of me being alive.

'I love you guys!' I said, and I didn't even care when they looked at me like I was the biggest loseroid in the whole wide world amen.

Frankie Teacup is dead

We walked up to my front door and I put the key in and turned it.

Sorry if that was a really boring sentence by the way.

I could tell something weird was going on as soon as I opened the door. Partly because I'm good at noticing things like that, but also because my dad was lying face down on the carpet, banging his fists against the floor, crying.

'Say it isn't so, Frankie!' he bawled, his favourite Frankie Teacup and the Saucers song playing on the radio.

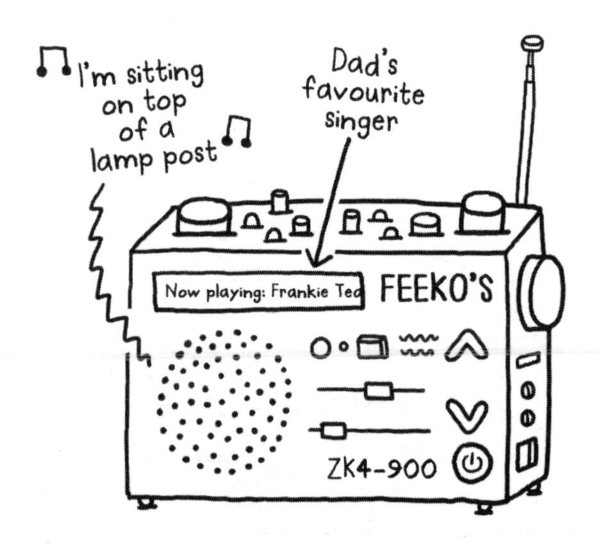

I walked up to my dad and tapped him on the shoulder with the end of my foot. 'What in the unkeelness is going on?' I said, feeling a bit embarrassed in front of Bunky and Nancy.

'Frankie Teacup is dead,' huffed my mum, pulling a ginormous suitcase down the stairs and plonking it on the carpet next to my dad.

'NOOOOOO!!!' screamed my dad, and I wondered if the suitcase had landed on his fingers.

'Oh get a grip, Kenneth,' said my mum, helping him sit up, and my dad stopped crying and started wiping tears away from his cheeks.

He peered up at Bunky and Nancy and did a wobbly-lipped smile. 'Looking forward to the weekend, guys?' he snuffled.

'Can't wait,' said Bunky, and we all got in the car and drove to Plonkton, with Frankie Teacup and the Saucers music playing the whole way there.

Are we nearly there yet?

You know how it says 'Are we nearly there yet?' in massive letters at the top of this page? That's what Bunky had just said.

'Not far now, Bunky,' said my mum, rummaging around in the bag by her feet. 'Cucumber?' she smiled, pulling the lid off a plastic tub and passing it through the gap between the seats.

'Why the keelness not,' I said, grabbing a slice and chomping it in half. 'Mmm, comperleeterly tasterless!' I spluttered, remembering something our dinner lady, Mrs Tumbles, told me once.

'Did you know that cucumbers are one hundred percent made out of water?' I said, feeling like the cleverest little Barry ever.

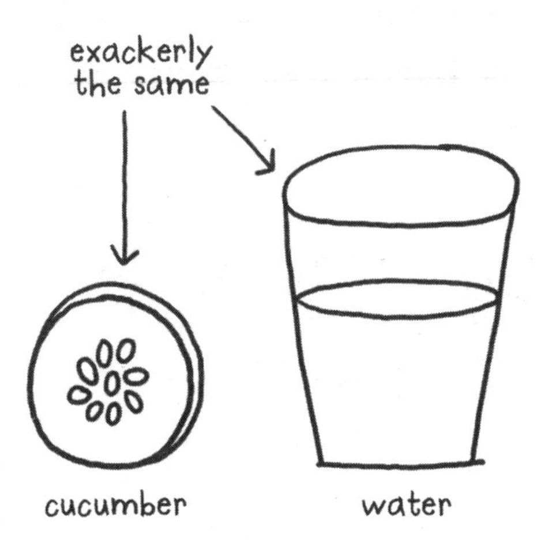

Nancy wrinkled her forehead and smiled. 'Wouldn't they just be water then?' she said, pointing at the skin bit and all the seeds, but I ignored her.

'Urrggh, I feel sick,' said Bunky, rolling his head over and leaning it on Nancy's shoulder.

'Eurghyuck, I feel sick too!' I said, putting my hands over my eyes so I didn't have to see.

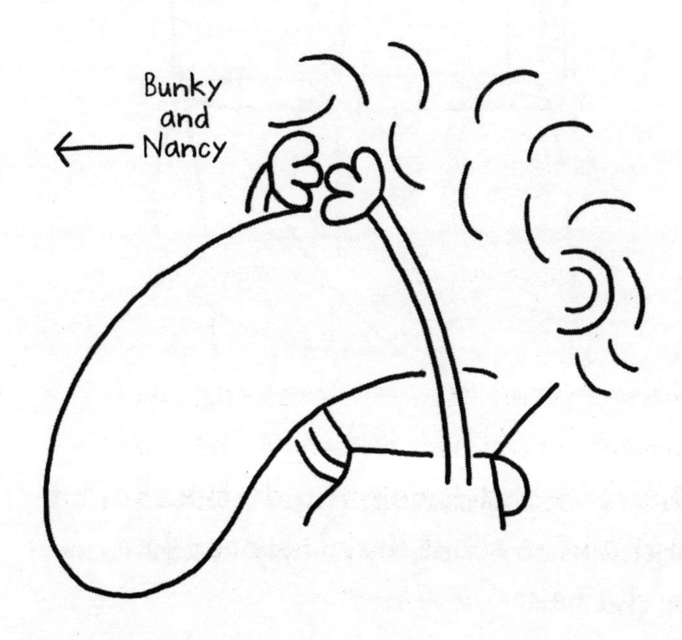

My mum stuck her face between the seats and did her worried face. 'Maybe we should pull over, Ken?' she said.

'No way!' I shouted, and I peeked through my fingers at my dad's eyes in the rear-view mirror.

'Oh Frankie, why did you have to go?' he wailed, and he started singing along to the Frankie Teacup and the Saucers song that was coming out of the speakers.

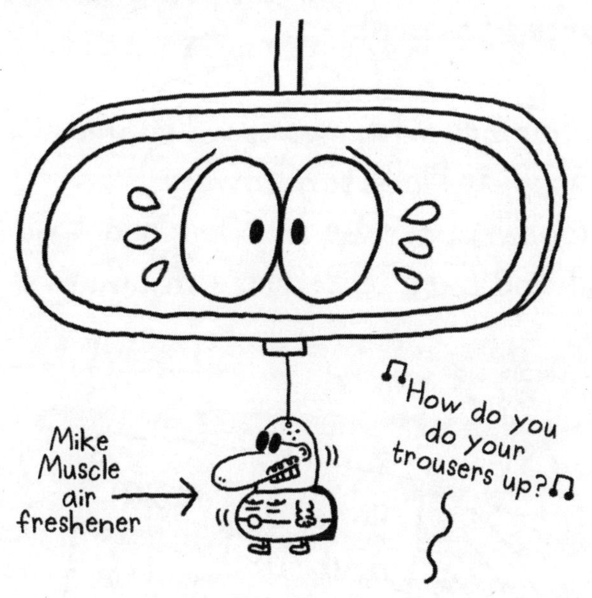

'Tell us something else about Plonkton, Barry!' said Nancy, winding down the window for Bunky and wafting air into his face.

I was just about to open my mouth and tell them how there were millions of benches in Plonkton for all the old grannies and grandads to sit down on, when my dad stopped his singing and started to speak.

'Remember when we saw Frankie Teacup at Plonkton Tower, Smoochypoos?' he sniffled, reaching his hand over to squeeze my mum's.

'Barry was just a twinkle in your eye back then!' smiled my mum, and they looked at each other, then at me.

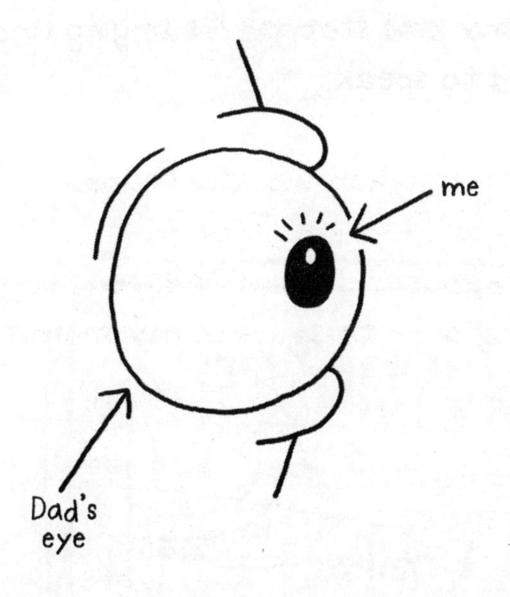

'NOW I'M DEFINITELY GOING TO BE SICK,' I said, wafting some of Bunky's air in my face, and I glanced out of the window and gasped.

'I spy something beginning with P!' I shouted, and I waggled my hand towards a sign.

Banana Moon

'Here we are!' said my dad as we finally drove up to the caravan. He was trying to sound cheerful, but everyone could tell he was still upset about Frankie Teacup.

'Don't worry Mr Loser,' said Bunky, leaning forwards and putting his hand on my dad's shoulder. 'I cried when my granny died, but now I can hardly even remember what she looks like!'

'Thanks for that, Bunky,' said my dad, and we all got out and stretched our legs.

It was comperleeterly dark outside apart from a sliver of moon up in the sky. 'Look Barry, a banana moon!' said my dad, and he started singing 'Banana Moon', which is one of Frankie Teacup's most famous songs.

I looked up at the banana moon and imagined it being the torn-off edge of a banana-flavour scratch-and-sniff sticker. I reached my hand out and tried to give it a scratch.

I put my finger up to my nose and breathed in, but it just smelled of finger, not at all like banana.

'Ahem, Kenneth? Are you going to let me carry this?' huffed my mum, dragging a suitcase up the slope to the caravan, and my dad stopped singing and wobbled off to help.

'So this is it, is it?' said Bunky, wheeling his suitcase through a puddle.

I turned round to face Bunky and Nancy and stretched my arms out wide. 'Welcome to Plonkton!' I boomed, and a drop of rain hit me in the eye.

'Is that your caravan?' said Nancy, and I nodded.

'Amazekeels, isn't it!' I said, grabbing my suitcase and staggering up to the caravan, following my nose into the bedroom that had the bunk bed in it. 'Bagsy the top bunk!' I said, even though I didn't really have to bagsy it, seeing as it was MY caravan.

'Where do I go?' said Nancy, looking at the two beds. I waggled my eyebrows and pulled a mattress out from under the bottom bunk.

'TA-DA!' I smiled, and Nancy shrugged.

Bunky jumped on to his bed and pulled a packet of Cola Flavour Not Birds out of his bag. 'We can share these for a midnight feast!' he said, grinning his three little grins at Nancy.

I looked up at my top bunk and suddenly wished I was on a bottom one, hanging out with Bunky and Nancy.

'But . . .' I said, and my but floated round the room like a butterfly chopped in half. Which was weird, because at that exact second I spotted a moth, fluttering round the light bulb.

Suddenly it swooped, heading straight for me. 'ARRGGGHHH!!!' I screamed, sticking fingers into all the holes in my face, just in case he fancied flying down one.

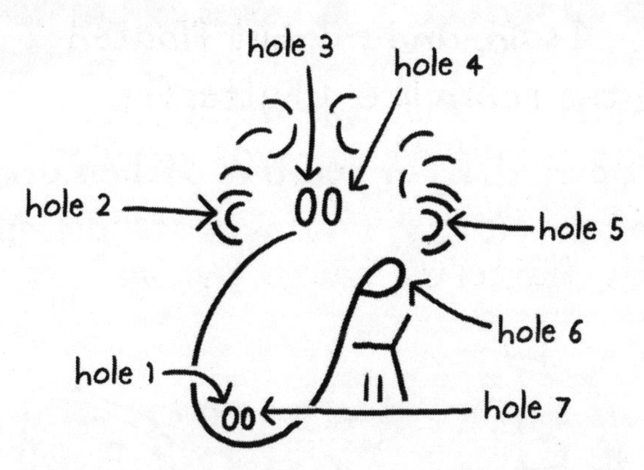

Nancy cupped her hands round the moth and plopped it out the window. 'I'm glad I've got you to protect me, Barry!' she giggled, and Bunky laughed.

'Very funny,' I smiled, and I leaped up on my bunk and started to enjoy my weekend.

The next morning

'Mornkeels!' I said, the millisecond my eyes opened. I jumped out of bed and landed on Nancy, who was still asleep.

'Ummpphh!' she blurted, waking up. 'Eurgh, thanks for that, Barry.' Her hair was sticking up from where she'd been sleeping, and she stroked it flat with her hand, like a cat.

Bunky yawned and opened his eyes, stretching his arms and legs like a dog. 'Mmmm, hello Nancy!' he smiled, and I stood there for a bit waiting for my hello too.

I pulled the curtains open and looked through the window. 'What a luvverly day!' I said, shutting them again.

We stumbled into the kitchen and sat down at the tiny table, waiting for my mum and dad to feed us breakfast.

'So what's the plan?' said Bunky, picking a pillow feather out of Nancy's hair and blowing it.

It flew straight up my nostril and I sneezed so loud the whole caravan shuddered.

'Has my Snookyflumps caught a chill?' said my mum, shuffling into the kitchen in her dressing gown and slippers. 'Kenneth! I told you this place was too cold!' she squawked, even though he was too busy singing in the shower to hear.

My mum kissed my head and gave it a little cuddle. 'I'M FINE,' I said, feeling all embarrassed in front of Bunky and Nancy.

'I remember bringing you to Plonkton when you were just a baby. Good as gold, you were!' she smiled, pulling the lid off her cucumber tub and chomping one in half. 'A lovely baby, Barry was,' she spluttered, plonking a box of Feeko's Bran Chunks on the table.

'Just ignore her,' I said, sticking my finger up my nose and waggling it around, looking for the pillow feather.

Bunky wrinkled his forehead and smiled at my mum. 'Erm, do you have any **Future Ratboy** Flakes?' he said. 'I don't really like these ones . . .'

'KENNETH!' screamed my mum. 'POP DOWN THE SHOPS AND GET BUNKY SOME FUTURE RATMAN CORNFLAKES, WOULD YOU!'

The shower stopped and we heard my dad crashing and banging in the room next door. 'What's that, my dear?' he said, appearing in the doorway with a towel wrapped round his waist.

I pulled my finger out of my nose and tried to blow the feather off, but it was too busy being stuck on by snot to move.

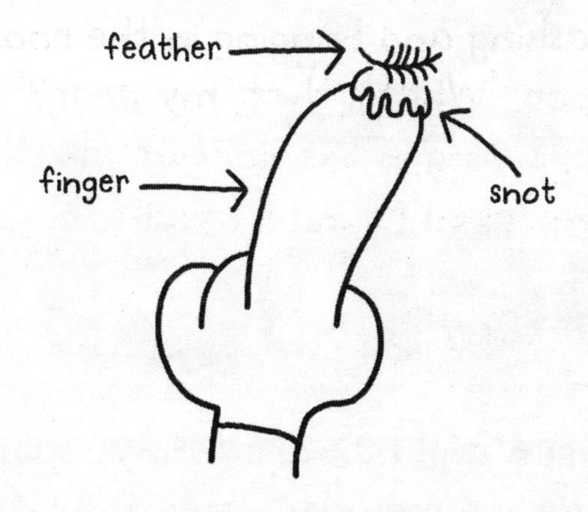

'Right, that's it,' I said, getting up and stomping to the door. I'd had enough of being embarrassed by my mum and dad for one day thank you very much indeed, plus I suddenly fancied a Cat Ear for breakfast. 'I'm going to Gino's!'

Bert the bench

'Your mum and dad are funny!' said Nancy, as we trundled down the hill.

I did a silent blowoff and gazed up at the sky. Clouds floated over like thought bubbles, except with raindrops inside them instead of words.

'They're not my real mum and dad, I'm adopted,' I lied, leading us towards a wire fence with a million trees behind it.

A sign saying 'CAUTION: BADGERS IN FOREST' was stuck into the ground, and Bunky sniggled.

'Ooh, badgers! I'm sooo scaredypoos!' he cackled, and we all snortled.

A spotty teenager I'd spotted on my last trip to Plonkton was leaning against one of the trees, holding a lead with a three-legged dog on the end of it.

'Mornkeels!' I said, showing off in front of Bunky and Nancy.

'Morn-keels? Who are you, **Future Ratboy**'s ugly brother?' laughed the teenager, and the dog barked, making me do one of my surprise blowoffs.

Bunky and Nancy giggled as I clambered over the fence into Badger Forest, trying to get away from my blowoff, which had been one of those really smelly ones. A dirt path zigzagged through the trees, all the way down to the sea. I picked up a twig and pointed it at a bench.

'See that bench?' I said, and Bunky and Nancy nodded. 'There's billions of them in Plonkton! They're for all the old people. They can't go five centimetres without a restypoos!'

Bunky bounded over to the bench and plonked his bum down. 'BORING!' he barked, blowing off into the planks, and Nancy giggled.

'NO IT'S NOT!' I said, snapping my twig in half, which is what I do when my sort of pet dog isn't listening to my Plonkton stories properly.

'"In memory of Bert, who liked a nice sit down",' said Nancy, reading what it said on the little plaque, and she sat down next to Bunky.

'Poor old Bert. All that's left of him now is this bench,' she sighed, and Bunky budged a little closer.

'Don't worry Nancy, he's got us keeping him warm,' he smiled, putting his arm around her shoulders, and I felt myself go queasy.

The whole time I'd known Bunky, I'd never seen him even look at a girl's shoulders. And now he had his ARM around some.

'Come on loseroids!' I said, pretending what had just happened hadn't just happened, and I headed off, my sort-of pet dog and cat following behind.

Plonkton seafront

We plopped out of Badger Forest and on to Plonkton seafront. 'Wait here!' I said, running up to a little van and buying three chocolate ice creams with the holiday money my mum had given me.

'Dog Poos all round!' I smiled, handing one to Bunky and one to Nancy. 'It's like the sky's doing blowoffs!' I chuckled, pointing at the wind, and an inside-out umbrella blew past, dragging an old granny with it.

Bunky scrunched his eyes up and stuffed his spare hand in its pocket. 'Bit cold for ice creams, isn't it?' he shivered, looking at Nancy. 'Let's go back to the caravan and read about kittens!'

'Don't be such a baby, it'll put hairs on your chest!' I said, copying what my dad always says when I start moaning.

'Oh great, a holiday in Granny Town AND hairs on my chest. Just what I've always wanted!' snortled Bunky, trying to make Nancy laugh, and I felt my nose droop like a melting ice cream.

I looked at Nancy to see if she was laughing at Bunky's joke, but she was too busy trying to see through her glasses, which looked like they could do with those windscreen wipers that **Future Ratboy**'s goggles have.

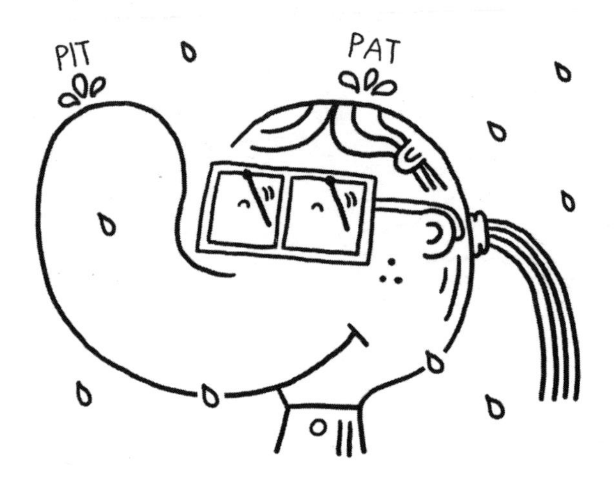

She slid them off her face and gave them a wipe with the corner of her sleeve. And that's when we heard the squawk.

A ginormerous seagull swooped down and snatched Nancy's glasses with its claws, flying off towards the sea.

'My glasses!' screamed Nancy, and she ran across the road, which wasn't as dangerous as it sounds, seeing as the only things allowed to drive down it are those really slow granny-mobiles.

'Be careful!' I shouted, running after her, and an old grandad in a granny-mobile skidded round me, crashing into a Fish and Chips shop at one centimetre per hour.

'I'll save you, Nancy!' cried Bunky, even though it was Nancy's glasses that needed saving, not her.
He jumped up in the air and waggled his legs around like someone in a cartoon, then zoomed off after the comperleeterly wrong bird.

The waves were crashing against the rocks as I plodded down the beach and caught up with Nancy. She waded into the water, reaching her arms out to sea, but it was too late. The seagull had turned into a dot.

'Forget it Nancy, it's too dangerous!' I shouted, licking my ice cream and grabbing her ponytail to pull her back. I looked around for Bunky and spotted a dog-shaped person bounding around halfway down the beach, chasing a pigeon.

'I-I can't see,' said Nancy, dropping to her knees and landing on a nice squidgy bit of seaweed, which was lucky, because pebbles can really hurt.

'I wish my mum was here,' she muttered, squinting up at me and looking like she might cry. 'She'd know what to do.'

I patted Nancy on the head and looked around on the off-chance Mrs Verkenwerken had got in her car and driven three hours to Plonkton seafront for a morning stroll along the beach.

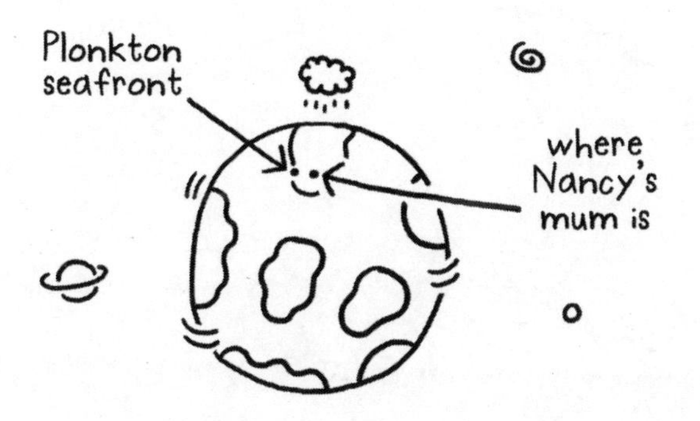

'How about some old granny instead?' I said, because there were millions of them staggering along with their walking sticks, stopping every three seconds for a nice sit down. But Nancy shook her head.

'Everything's blurry and I want to go home,' she cried.

I put my spare hand on my hip and wondered what to do. Then Bunky bounded towards us, his tongue waggling out of his mouth. 'What's happened? Is my Nancy Wancy OK?' he barked, skidding to a stop.

'Nancy Wancy?' I said, wrinkling my forehead, but Bunky just ignored me.

'I can't see, Bunky,' whimpered Nancy, and Bunky pushed past me, helping her to her feet.

'I'll be your eyes, Nancy,' he said, putting his hand on her head, and he guided her back towards the road.

Outside Gino's Pizza

I finished my ice cream and started running after Bunky and Nancy. 'Wait for me! I can lead you to Gino's!' I said, even though they were already standing right in front of it. I looked up at my favourite pizza restaurant in the whole wide world amen and scrinched my eyes into little grins.

The whole building was in the shape of a pizza, with windows all the way round and a massive twizzling 'GINO'S PIZZA' sign stuck on top. Outside the front door was a wooden cut-out of Gino, holding a plate of Cat Ears.

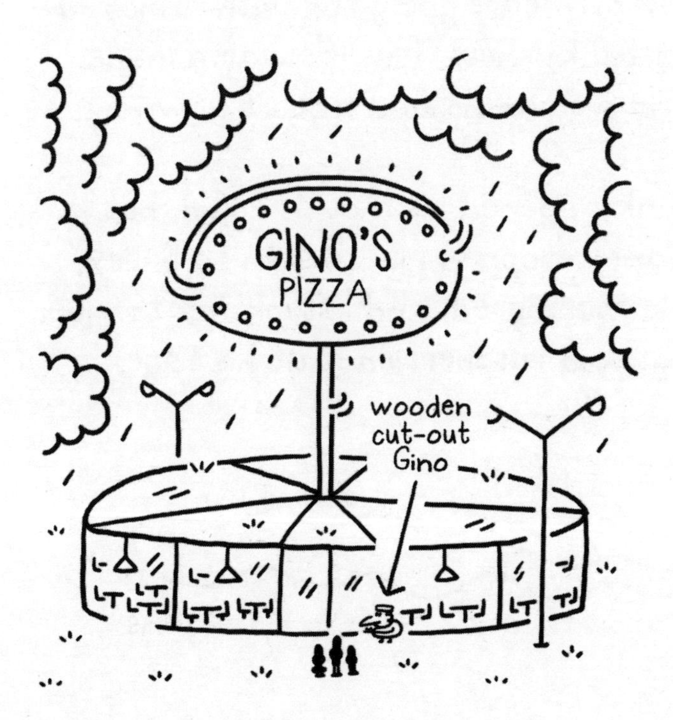

Bunky turned to me and did my mum's worried face. 'Nancy's had a terrible shock, Barry. The last thing she needs is one of Gino's Cat Feet,' he said.

'They're Cat EARS,' I snapped, feeling my own ears going red with annoyed-at-Bunky-ness. 'Plus it's warm inside, and we can have a nice sit down . . .'

Bunky opened his mouth again, but Nancy stopped him. 'Listen to Barry,' she murmured, and I stuck my tongue out and raspberried it at his face.

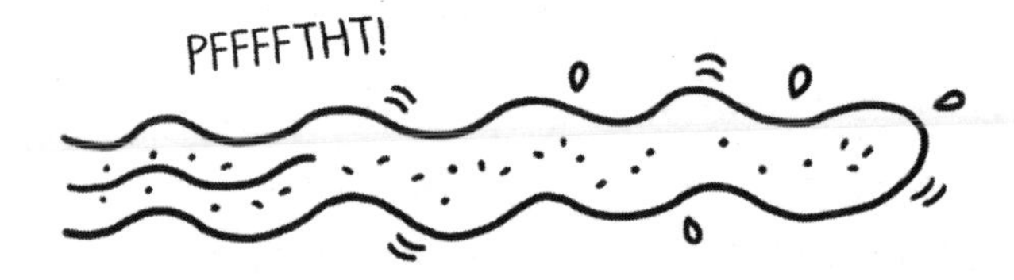

Inside Gino's Pizza

The bell above the door clanged as we walked into Gino's. 'A plate of Cat Ears and three Fronkeels over hee-yer!' I shouted, which is what I shout when I'm comperleeterly showing off.

'Barry, is that you?' crackled a tiny old voice from the kitchen that sounded exackerly like Gino's, probably because it was.

I sat down in my favourite booth and looked up at Bunky and Nancy. 'Isn't this the keelest!' I beamed.

'I just wish I could see it properly,' said Nancy, shuffling her bum along until she was opposite me. She patted her hands around on the table to find the menu and held it up to her face, squinting at the words.

Bunky squidged in next to her and looked around. He ran his finger along the table and held it up, peering at the clump of dust sitting on the end of it like an ancient bogie, and he did his face he does when he doesn't like something.

I felt my nose droop again, disappointed that he wasn't excited about Gino's, then felt it undroop, because I'd just spotted the real-life Gino.

'Well, well, well, if it isn't my favourite customer in the whole wide world!' Gino croaked, peering through his glasses as he shuffled towards us at one millimetre per hour. He was carrying a plate of Cat Ears and three cans of Cherry Fronkle. 'My, how you've grown!' he smiled, even though I comperleeterly hadn't.

'Is that Gino?' said Nancy. 'What does he look like, Bunky? Is he as keel as Barry says?'

Bunky looked at Gino and wrinkled his whole face up. 'Erm . . .' he mumbled, and I kicked his leg, just in case he was about to say something horrible.

'How's business, Gino?' I said, grabbing a Cat Ear and stuffing it in my mouth. 'Mmm, it's like eating a real-life cat's ear, except not as hairy and disgustering!' I spluttered, bits of Cat Ear splattering all over Bunky and Nancy's faces.

'Oh Barry, business isn't good at all,' warbled Gino, squinting through his glasses at the empty restaurant. 'Nobody comes to Gino's any more,' he said, and I looked around, trying to see what the problem was.

A photo of Gino and his wife standing outside their house hung on the wall at an angle. The glass in its frame was all cracked.

The chair underneath it wobbled in the wind of a ceiling fan, probably because it only had three legs, a bit like that dog from Badger Forest earlier.

Vases sat on the tables with dead flowers drooping out of them, and I spotted a petal on the floor, stuck in a puddle of dried-up Cherry Fronkle.

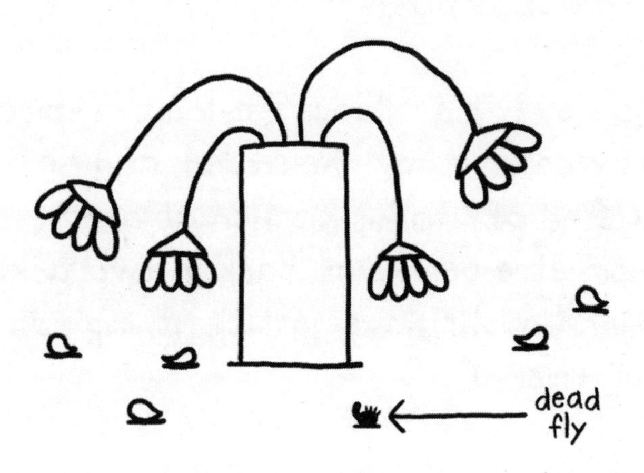

'What if Gino's isn't as keel as I thought it was?' I thought to myself.

I did my sad face and tried to think of something to say that wouldn't hurt Gino's feelings. 'Ooh, that reminds me,' I smiled, even though it hadn't reminded me at all. 'These are my friends, Bunky and Nancy. Bunky's sort of like my pet dog, and Nancy's glasses just got snatched out of her hand by a seagull, so now she's blind.'

Gino's eyes did a loop-the-loop. 'Typical Barry Loser story!' he smiled, and he shuffled off to his kitchen at one centimetre per hour. 'Back in two ticks! I think I might have just the thing for your friend!'

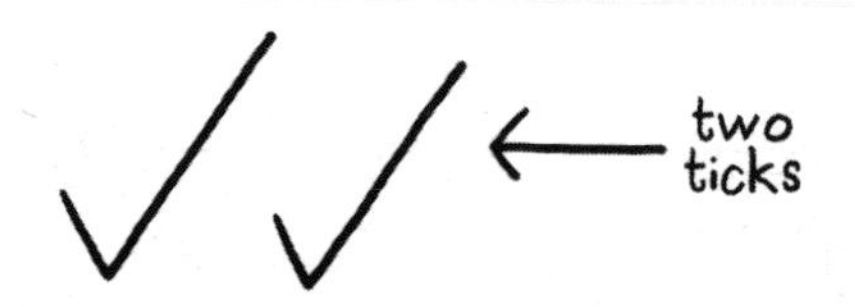

Mrs Gino's granny glasses

'Thanks for the specs, Gino!' beamed Nancy half an hour later, wobbling out of Gino's Pizza wearing Mrs Gino's old granny glasses, which Mrs Gino didn't need any more, seeing as she'd comperleeterly turned into a bench last year.

I led Bunky and Nancy down to the sea and pointed my finger at a rock sticking out of the water that looked exackerly like an elbow.

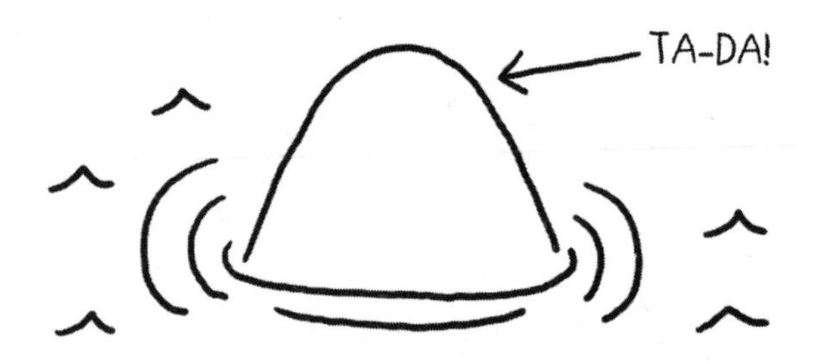

'See that rock? It's called Elbow Rock!' I smiled, and Nancy squinted through her granny glasses, looking unimpressed.

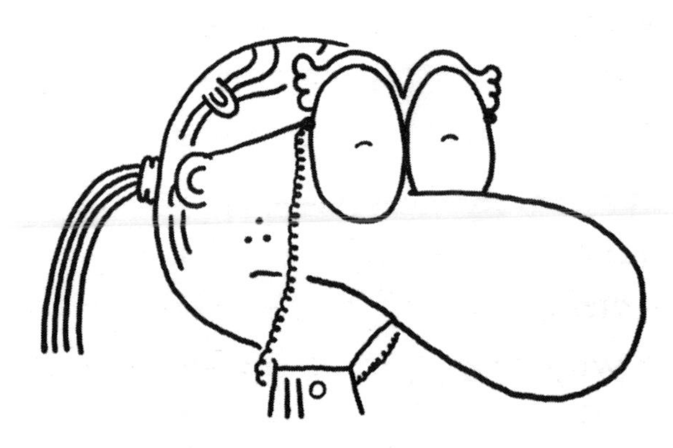

'Don't loads of rocks look like elbows?' said Bunky, pulling his sleeve up and looking at his elbow, just to check.

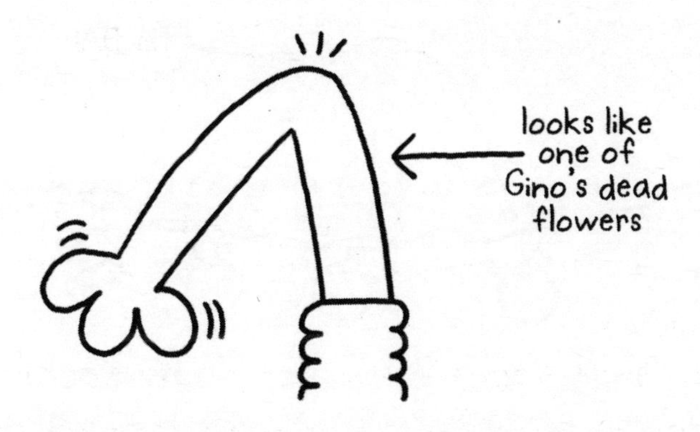

I ignored Bunky and carried on with my tour of Plonkton, which included Plonkton Tower, where my mum and dad saw Frankie Teacup live in concert eight million years ago, and the world famous Plonkton Lights, which are these amazaloid light bulbs that go the whole way along Plonkton seafront.

Annoyingly it was still daytime though, so really all we were looking at was loads of switched-off light bulbs swaying in the wind.

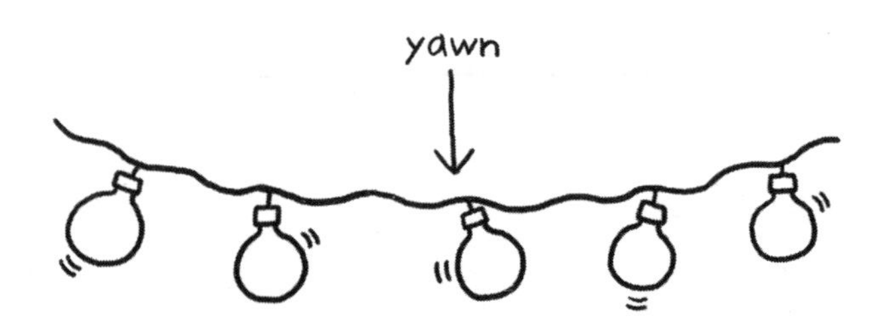

'Who's this, Nancy?' sniggled Bunky, as we walked back up the hill to my caravan an hour later. He hunched his back and shuffled along, pretending to hold a plate of Cat Ears and three cans of Fronkle. 'My name is Gino and I've just done a massive blowoff!' he warbled.

I felt my ears start to go red. I'd had enough of Bunky showing off in front of Nancy, and I didn't like the way he was talking about Gino. 'What HAS got into you, Bunky?' I shouted, even though I'd already worked it out.

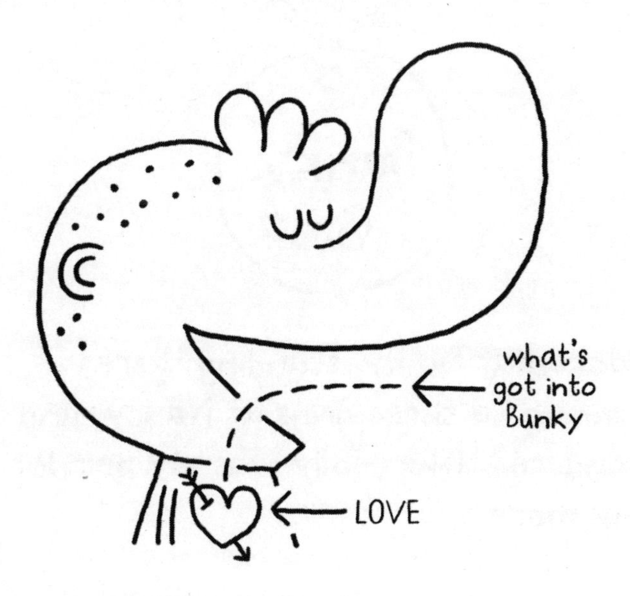

'You're a bad dog!' I said, wagging my finger at him and walking ahead.

'I'm not a dog, I'm Gino!' he barked, and the words swam down my earholes into my legs, making them go wobbly.

I looked at Bunky, standing there grinning his three grins at Nancy, and wondered if he really was my pet dog any more.

And that's when I heard a familiar voice.

Mister Whatsitcalled

'Coowee, Barry!' said Mr Whatsitcalled, the man who owns the caravan next door to ours whose name I can never remember.

'Oh, hi Mr . . .' I mumbled, leaving the Whatsitcalled bit off. He was holding a massive pot of pink paint and dipping a brush into it, sploshing it on to the side of his caravan, which used to be yellow.

Nancy waggled her new specs and wrinkled her forehead, trying to make me and Bunky laugh. 'Is it these glasses or is that old man painting his caravan pink?' she said, and Bunky sniggled.

'This place gets more ridiculoserous by the millisecond! Come on Nancy Wancy, let's go read our kitten book,' he chuckled, and he put his arm round her shoulders and started walking towards my caravan.

One of the problems with being excited about reading a kitten book is that you don't look where your feet are going. 'WAHHH!!!' screamed Bunky, slipping in a pile of badger poo.

He flipped into the air like someone in a cartoon and crashed into Mr Whatsitcalled's just-painted caravan.

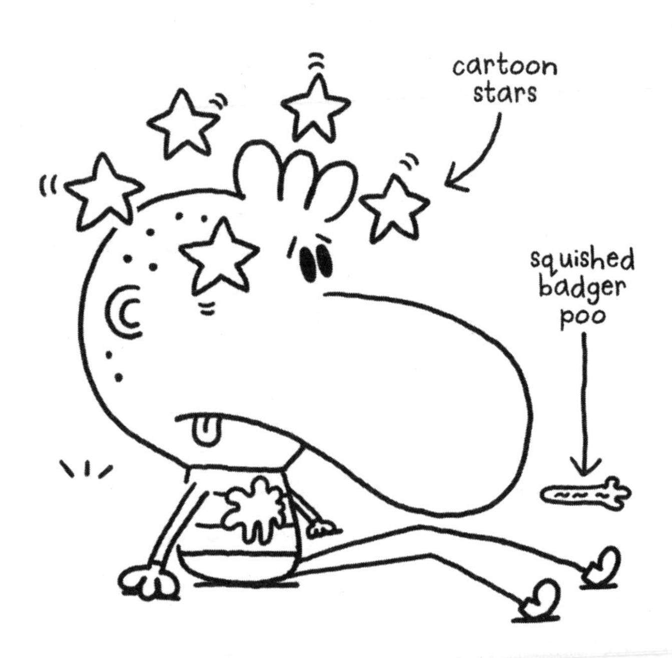

'My jumper! It's all pink!' he shrieked, as Nancy helped him off the floor and up the stairs into the caravan.

'Sorry about your friend's jumper, Barry,' said Mr Whatsitcalled, painting over the bit Bunky had just crashed into, and I shrugged, wondering if a real friend would walk off to read a kitten book without even inviting you along.

'Oh, he's not my real friend. I was just adopting him for a bit,' I said, and I heard a cackle from behind me that didn't sound like Mr Whatsitcalled at all. I turned my head round all slowly, and gasped and blew off at the same time, which is never a good idea.

Standing right in front of me was Sharonella.

Sharonella has arrived

'WHAT IN THE NAME OF UNKEELNESS?!' I screamed, running back towards Badger Forest, my shorts falling down from how much my legs were waggling.

'I'm not gonna eat you, Bazza!' cackled Sharonella, as I tumbled to the ground.

'How in the why what when?' I blurted, lying in a puddle with my shorts round my ankles.

'Thought I'd come and see Plonkton wiv me own eyes, seeing as you were going on about it the whole time,' smiled Sharonella, picking up a twig and snapping it in half. 'My gran likes her fish and chips so she was like, "Yeah, why not, Shaz, let's go down for the day!"'

I stood up and looked around for Sharonella's granny and spotted her talking to my mum outside our caravan.

'I knew you were staying in a caravan. All we had to do was drive around for five hours looking in all the windows,' grinned Sharonella, and she threw her half-a-twig at a tree.

'OW!' said a voice from behind the tree, and I jumped, coming up with one of my brilliant and amazekeel jokes while still in mid-air.

'Argh, a talking tree, let's leave!' I said, waiting for Sharonella to wee herself with laughter like Bunky would have done, back in the good old days before he started fancying Nancy. 'LEAVE, get it? Trees have leaves!' I grinned.

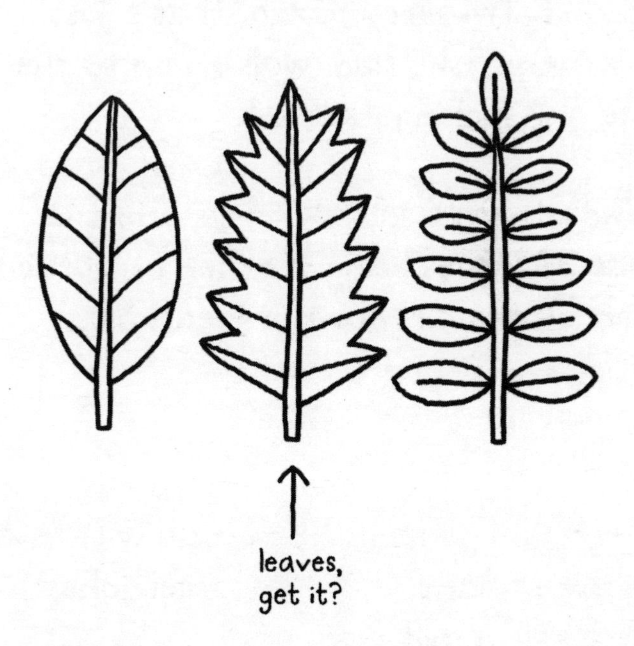

Sharonella wrinkled her forehead and looked at me like I was a comperleet loseroid. 'I'm sorry Bazza, that's just not funny,' she said, walking up to the tree and kicking its trunk.

'Who's there?' said the tree, and the noise of leaves being trodden on rustled through the air, down my earholes.

Trev or Trevor

Five legs walked out from behind the tree, two of them belonging to that spotty teenager with the three-legged dog from earlier.

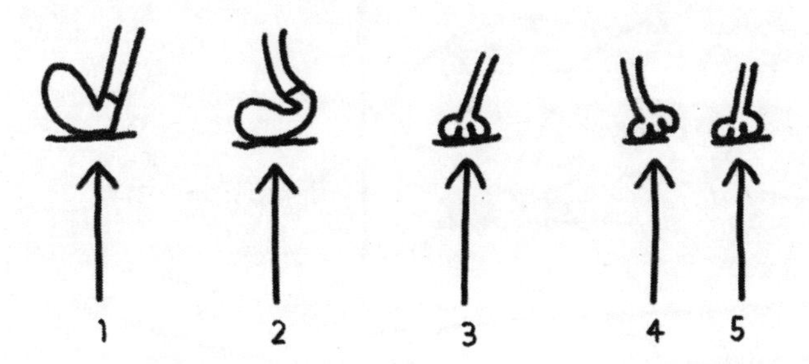

'Name's Trevor. Trev to my friends,' he said, and I wondered if that meant I should call him Trev or Trevor.

'I'm Sharonella, but you can call me Shaz. And him over there's Bazza,' said Sharonella, pointing at me. Trev or Trevor stared at me like I was for sale in a Feeko's window.

'My name is Barry, actually,' I said, because my name is NOT Bazza.

'Barry Actually? That's a weird name!' said Trev or Trevor, cracking up at his own stupid joke.

'Now THAT'S funny!' snortled Sharonella, and I rolled my eyes, bending down to pull my shorts up, which had been round my ankles this whole time, in case you didn't know.

When I stood back up, Trev or Trevor had run off and Sharonella and the dog with three legs were running after him.

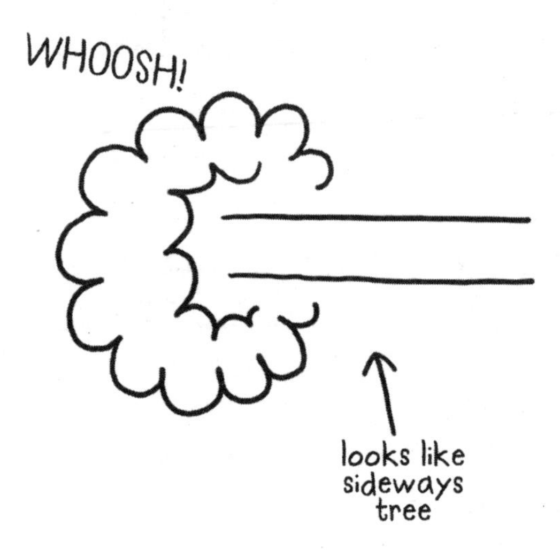

'Where are we going?' I screamed, zooming past a sign saying 'TOILETS THIS WAY', so I guessed we must be going to the toilets. 'You must really need a wee!' I said, once I'd caught up with them.

Trev or Trevor snortled and nudged Sharonella. 'Who invited him?' he laughed, nodding at me.

'Ahh don't, Trev, Bazza's all right!' she smiled, and I wondered how they'd suddenly become so friendly seeing as we'd only met him two milliseconds ago and all they'd done is run to a toilet together. Trev or Trevor opened his mouth and I counted seven fillings.

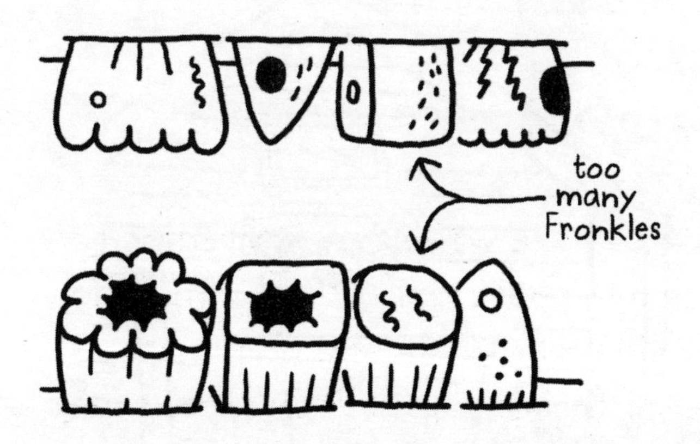

'Who wants to see summink disgusting?' he whispered, and we both nodded.

Stinksplats

We followed Trev or Trevor round the back of the toilet block and watched as he climbed on a bin and lifted up a window flap. He stuck his head through and wriggled into the building.

'Why's Trev or Trevor climbing through that window when there's a perfectly keel door round the front?' I whispered to Sharonella, but she just ignored me, jumping on the bin and sticking her head through too.

'POOWEE!' she shouted, and she slipped in, legs waggling. 'Come on, Bazza!' echoed her voice, and I clambered on to the bin.

'Wossamatter, you scared, Bazza?' said Trev or Trevor's voice, and I stuck my head through the window. Him and Sharonella were standing in a tiny storeroom, surrounded by towers of toilet rolls and ginormous bottles of bleach.

The door to the storeroom was locked from the other side, and I nodded to myself like my mum's favourite detective, realising why we were going through the window.

'Wipe that frown off your face!' cackled Trev or Trevor, waggling a mop up my nostrils, and I immediakeely stopped nodding my head.

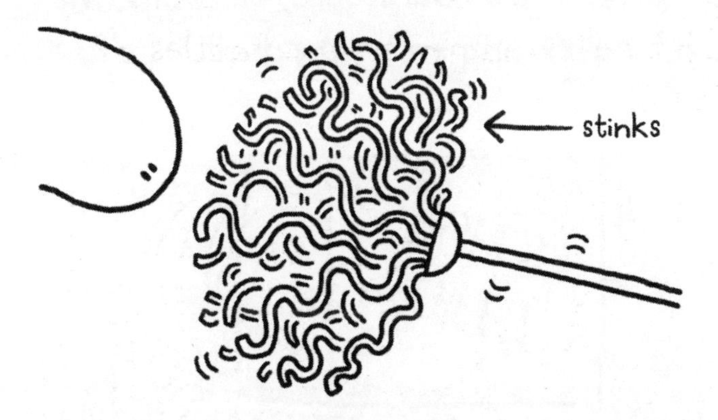

'BLEURGGHH!' I screamed, pushing away the mop, which stank a bit like cheese and kangaroos mixed together, unfunnily enough. 'What are you doing?' I said, pretending I was interested when all I really wanted to do was go back to the caravan and see what my ex-sort-of pet dog and cat were up to.

'Where are we going? What are we doing? You're like my baby bruvver!' laughed Trev or Trevor, picking up an empty cardboard box and putting it on his head. 'MUST. KILL. ALL. BAZZAS,' he said, pretending to be a robot.

Sharonella screamed with laughter, and I felt my ears go red, because I don't like it when someone who likes my nose laughs at someone else's jokes. 'Where's this disgusting thing then, Trev?' she said, sitting down on a box with URINAL SOAPS written on the side.

Trev or Trevor's eyebrows waggled as he ripped open a packet of toilet rolls and pulled one out. 'Hold that,' he said, passing it to Sharonella and kicking the mop bucket into the middle of the tiny room, brown frothy gunk-water sploshing on to the floor.

'POOWEE!' I said, realising why Sharonella had said it earlier.

'Nurse, hand me the toilet roll!' said Trev or Trevor, and Sharonella passed it to him, doing a curtsey. 'Ladies and Gentlebazzas, get ready to behold the world-famous STINKSPLAT!' cried Trev or Trevor, dunking the toilet roll into the bucket.

He lifted his hand out of the bucket and held up the soaking wet toilet roll, brown gunk-water dripping down his arm. 'Looks like a dead rat!' screeched Sharonella.

Then I felt something lick my leg.

'WAAHHH!!!' I screamed, pulling my head out of the window and doing a little dance on the bin lid.

SPLAT! splatted a wodge of soggy brown paper, hitting the inside of the window, right where my head had just been. 'Phew, that was lucky!' I said to myself, and I fell through the bin lid.

Bargain Barry

'Isn't this stealing?' I said, wiping bin-muck off my T-shirt. Trev or Trevor and Sharonella had wriggled back out of the window carrying the gunk-bucket and a jumbo pack of toilet rolls.

'Not if your dad owns the caravan site,' said Trev or Trevor proudly, and Sharonella gasped, looking impressed.

'Oh my days Trev, you must be a billionaire!' she grinned, nudging him, and I felt myself feeling a tiny bit jealous, even though I wasn't at all.

Trev or Trevor squinted his eyes, looking at me like I was for sale in Feeko's window again. 'Blimey Barry Actually, you're cheap!' he snarfled, pointing at my T-shirt.

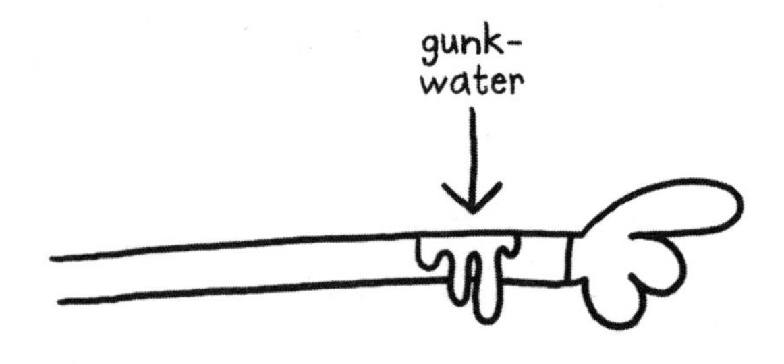

I looked down and spotted a price tag stuck on to it, probably from that bin I'd just fallen into.

The price tag was stuck right where you'd stick a scratch-and-sniff sticker, and had '23p' written on it.

'What a bargain!' said Sharonella, walking over and looping her arm through mine. 'I'll take him!'

'Waste of money if you ask me,' said Trev or Trevor, and he picked up the gunk-bucket. 'Now, let's see what you two are made of!'

Attack of the Stinksplats

It was getting dark as we tiptoed over to where all the caravans were, carrying the gunk-bucket and all the toilet rolls. I peered over at my caravan and spotted Sharonella's granny and my mum through the window, having a cup of tea and a slice of cucumber.

'See that caravan over there?' whispered Trev or Trevor from the notice board we were hiding behind, and we peered over at about seventeen caravans.

'Which one?' I whispered, feeling all naughty. It was actually quite fun being away from goody-goody Bunky and Nancy with their stupid scratch-and-sniff stickers, talking about kitten books the whole time.

'That one!' whispered Trev or Trevor, pointing at a rusty green caravan that was half falling apart. 'That's where the weird old man lives!'

Me and Sharonella looked at each other and waggled our eyebrows. 'Weird Old Man!' she mouthed, and I gulped, imagining an old man who was weird. 'What're we gonna do, Trev?' she whispered, holding on to his arm.

Trev or Trevor ripped a handful of paper off a toilet roll and dunked it into the bucket, and gunk-stink floated up my nostrils. 'THIS!' he shouted, throwing the stinksplat.

SPLAT! splatted the stinksplat, right on to one of Weird Old Man's windows. 'Bullseye!' shrieked Sharonella. 'My turn!' she whispered, ripping off a handful and dunking it in the gunk. 'Take that, Weird Old Man!'

Sharonella's stinksplat shot towards the clouds like a firework made out of poo, except instead of exploding in mid-air it landed on Weird Old Man's roof with a thud.

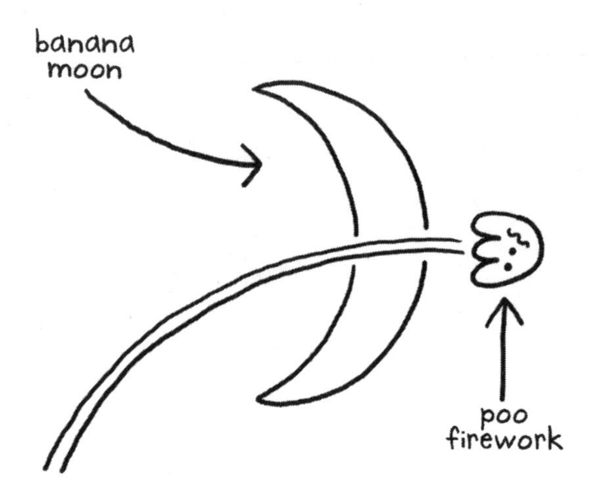

'I like a lady who can throw!' laughed Trev or Trevor, punching Sharonella on the arm, and she went the same colour as that pink frilly bikini in Feeko's window.

'I want a go!' I said, feeling all left out. Sharonella passed me a handful of toilet roll and I held it above the gunk-bucket, wondering if I should really be throwing stinksplats at the caravan of someone I didn't even know.

I glanced over at my caravan and spotted Bunky and Nancy through the bedroom window, laughing and chomping on Cola Flavour Not Birds.

Then I looked at Sharonella, Trev or Trevor and the dog with three legs and wondered if they could be my new sort-of pet cat and dogs. They were definitely more exciting than my stupid old ones. Plus one of them was an actual real-life dog.

'What's wrong Barry Actually, you scared?' grinned Trev or Trevor, and I closed my eyes and dunked my hand into the gunk.

Weird Old Man

One of the annoying things about being me is how comperleeterly rubbish at throwing I am. I pulled my arm back and got ready for Sharonella and Trev or Trevor to start laughing.

The stinksplat whooshed out of my hand like a dead rat shooting out of a cannon. 'Oh my days Bazza, it's heading straight for the door!' gasped Sharonella, and I wondered if maybe I was only rubbish at throwing when Bunky was around.

'YIPPEE-KEEL-KAYAY!' I screamed, and my eyes loop-the-looped as the stinksplat got closer and closer to Weird Old Man's front door. Which was unsuddenly . . . beginning . . . to . . . OPEN.

'I'm out of here!' said Trev or Trevor, running off, and Sharonella and the three-legged dog zoomed after him. I tried to turn and follow them, but I couldn't move.

One of my legs wished its owner had never thrown the stinksplat in the first place, while the other one was having the keelest fun ever.

The door opened and a familiar looking person appeared. I Future-Ratboy-zoomed my eyes in and gasped. Standing in the doorway wasn't a weird old man at all. It was Gino from Gino's Pizza.

'WHAT IN THE NAME OF UNKEELNESS?!' I screamed, as the stinksplat exploded in his face.

Melty cheese face

Gino wiped the stinksplat off his glasses and peered at me. 'B-Barry?' he gasped, his whole face melting like the cheese on a boiling hot Cat Ear.

I stared at Gino, my mouth hanging open. 'What's he doing living in a caravan?' I mumbled, thinking of the photo of him and Mrs Gino outside their house. Then I remembered how empty Gino's Pizza had been. 'Maybe Gino had to sell his house . . .' I whispered to myself in my detective voice.

'Poor Gino,' I muttered. He was wearing his uniform and looked like he was heading back to the restaurant to open up for the evening.

'I-I thought we were friends, Barry,' said Gino, sounding like my mum when she's really disappointed with me. He closed the door and started walking off.

'But . . .' I said, trying to explain how it was all Trev or Trevor's fault for making me throw the stinksplat. Then I remembered myself shouting 'YIPPEE-KEEL-KAYAY!' like I was having the best time ever.

A moth fluttered past in the banana moonlight and I watched it land on a nearby leaf and do a tiny poo.

I glanced up again, but Gino had turned into a dot.

Yellow granny tent

When I got back to my caravan, Sharonella was lying on a sun lounger, slurping a Cherry Fronkle like nothing had happened. I glanced around for Trev or Trevor and his three-legged dog, but they'd comperleeterly disappeared.

'What took you so long?' smiled Sharonella, looking at my shaking legs, but I just ignored her. I was too busy staring at a bright-yellow tent that had popped up right next to the caravan.

'What in the name of Mr Whatsitcalled is THAT?' I said.

'It's my granny's!' beamed Sharonella. 'Your mum said we could pitch up. Looks like we're staying the night, Bazza!' she burped, batting her eyelashes and smiling at my nose.

I stuck my head inside the tent and blinked. The whole world had suddenly gone yellow, even though it felt grey. 'Oh Shazza, I've been the naughtiest Bazza ever,' I said, crawling in.

'What's wrong, Bazzypoos?' said Sharonella, leaping off the sun lounger and clambering after me, putting her arm around my shoulders. I thought of Gino's melty cheese face and felt my bottom lip start to wobble.

'I hate to interrupt you two lovebirds, but who fancies some dinner?' said a voice that sounded exackerly like my dad's. I stuck my head out of the tent and blinked again.

Him and my mum had appeared with Sharonella's granny and my ex-sort-of pet dog and cat. Bunky was holding Nancy's kitten book and picking bits of dried-up pink paint off his jumper.

'We are NOT lovebirds!' I shouted, shrugging Sharonella's arm off my shoulder and crawling out of the tent, and we all started walking down to Plonkton seafront for dinner, hopefully not at Gino's.

Free puppies

We'd been walking for about half a minute, me with my eyes facing the floor so I didn't have to look at Bunky, when Nancy opened her mouth and gasped. 'Ooh, free puppies, Barry!' she said, tapping me on the shoulder, right where I'd just shrugged Sharonella's arm off it.

'How excitypoos,' I said, not even lifting my head up. I knew what she was doing, trying to get me in a good mood again by pretending there were free puppies for sale on the side of the road.

Sharonella scuttled over and started pulling on the leg of my shorts. 'She's not pulling yer leg Bazza, there really is a sign!' she squawked.

'OW-AH! GET OFF ME!' I shouted, waggling the leg she was pulling, and my mum stopped walking and twizzled round.

'BARRY!' she shouted, her eyes glaring straight through mine and into my brain, trying to work out why her little Barry was in such a bad mood.

'Sharonella is our guest tonight, and Losers DO NOT shout at their guests. Now, apologise,' she said, and I flomped my head over so I was looking at Sharonella.

'I'm . . .' I said, and I was just about to say the word 'sorry' as quietly as possible when I spotted a sign on the side of the road, in front of a ginormerous red caravan.

'FREE PUPPIES!' I squealed, jumping in the air and waggling my legs like someone in a cartoon.

Threelegs

Underneath the sign was a photo of a familiar-looking three-legged dog, sitting next to another dog and eight million tiny little puppies.

I Future-Ratboy-zoomed my eyes in and gasped. 'It's Trev or Trevor's dog!' I said, reading the writing next to the photo, which said this:

> **Our dogs, Threelegs and Pompom, have had puppies and we don't want any of them. Please call 555 4745 for your free one! £10 each.**

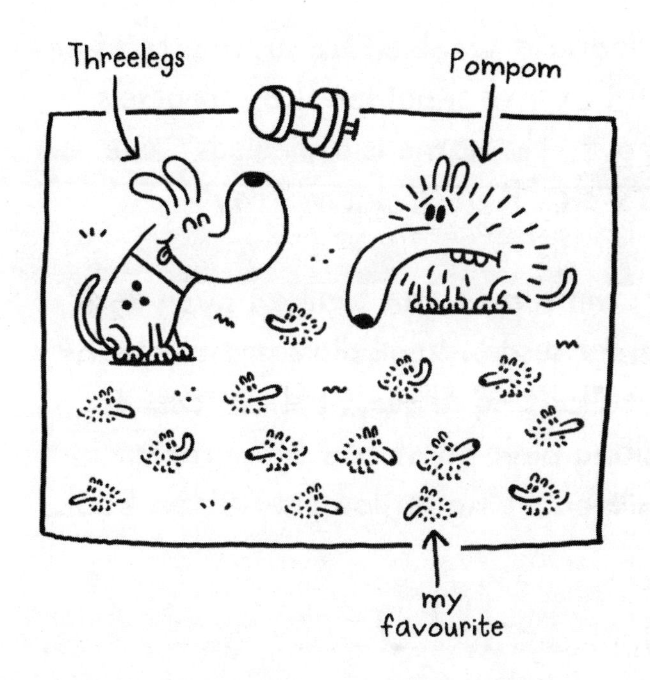

I looked at the ginormerous red caravan and squinted my eyes. 'So this must be Trev or Trevor's house,' I said to myself in my detective voice, remembering how he'd kind of made me throw a stinksplat right into my favourite pizza-restaurant-owner's face.

Sharonella wobbled up and rested her head on my shoulder like a Brussels sprout. 'His name is Threelegs?' she laughed. 'That is classic Trev!'

My mum and dad walked over with Nancy and Sharonella's granny. Bunky was floating around behind them, picking pink paint off his jumper while carrying his loserish kitten book.

'Can I get one Mum? Can I get one Mum? Can I get one Mum? Can I get one Mum?' I started saying. My plan was to keep on saying 'Can I get one Mum?' until I got one, even if it took my whole entire life amen.

'Sounds like somebody wants a puppy!' smiled Sharonella's granny, as the door of the ginormerous red caravan opened.

Trev or Trevor appeared, standing next to his mum. She had a baby strapped to her front and Trev was holding what looked like a real-life, squirming stinksplat. 'This what you're looking for?' he grinned, lifting up the tiny puppy.

'Ooh, isn't he adorable!' warbled my mum, wobbling straight past Trev or Trevor and up to the baby. 'Yes you are, aren't you! Yes you are!'

'Can I get a puppy, Mumsy? Pleeeease, I'll do anything!' I cried, wishing she'd stop going on about babies the whole time and concentrate on what was really important.

'What do you reckon, Mum?' said my dad, even though my mum's name isn't Mum, it's Maureen. He reached over and lifted the puppy out of Trev or Trevor's hands. 'We could call him Frankie Teacup!' he smiled, and a tear rolled down his cheek.

My mum stopped cooing over the baby and looked at my dad and me, standing there like the best little Barry and Kenneth Losers ever.

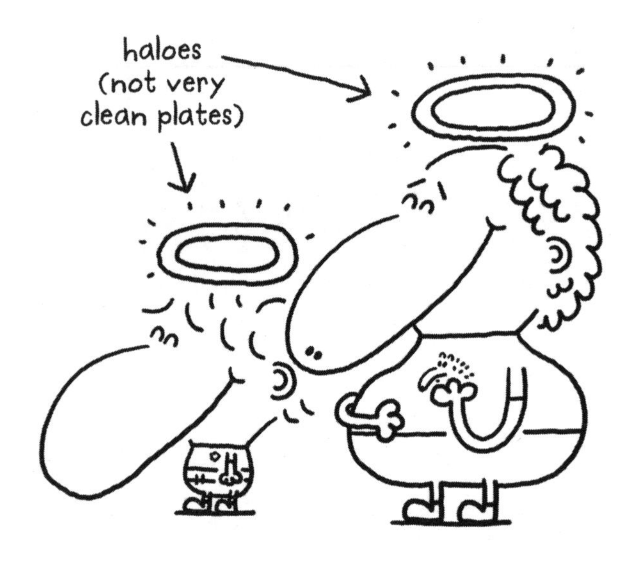

'Go on, Mrs Loser!' said Sharonella, poking my mum's thigh, and her granny tapped her on the head and put her finger up to her mouth.

'Pleeeease, Mum!' I begged, dropping to my knees. My mum shook her head to herself and smiled, and I held my breath.

I'd seen my mum shake her head to herself and smile before, and it usually meant she was about to say yes to something she thought was comperleeterly stupid. She opened her mouth and my whole body went wobbly. 'Why the coolness not!' she chuckled.

Bad Barry

'So we can pick the puppy up tomorrow?' I said for the billionth time as we walked down the hill to Plonkton seafront, and my mum nodded.

'Here we are,' said my dad, as we turned a corner into the car park of Gino's Pizza, and I blew off and gasped at the same time, which is never a good idea, especially when the wind is blowing your blowoff right towards your mouth.

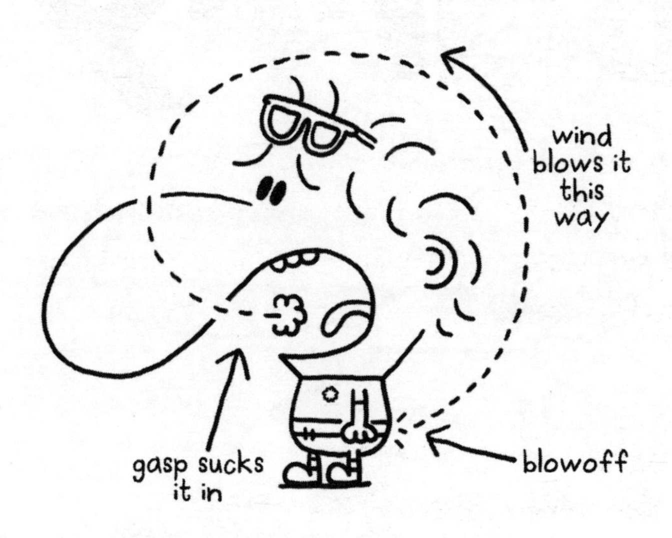

I'd been so excited about the free puppies that I'd comperleeterly forgotteren about Gino.

'W-we don't want to go here again, do we?' I said, spotting Gino sitting alone on his three-legged chair, and my heart wrinkled up like that bubblegum on the wall of Feeko's Supermarket. My dad swivelled his head round and loop-the-looped his eyes.

'Was it my hearing aid playing up or did you just say you didn't want to go to Gino's?' he said, even though he doesn't have a hearing aid.

'Oh, you know . . . I've already had Cat Ears once today,' I smiled, my face going the same colour as the paint on Bunky's jumper.

'Yeah, and it's all dusty and falling apart in there!' said Bunky, showing off in front of Nancy and everyone else.

My ears went red and twizzled round, along with the rest of my head. 'That's enough out of you!' I shouted, and I was just about to tell him he was a bad doggy when I realised something. Tomorrow I'd be getting a real-life puppy. I didn't need my sort-of pet dog any more.

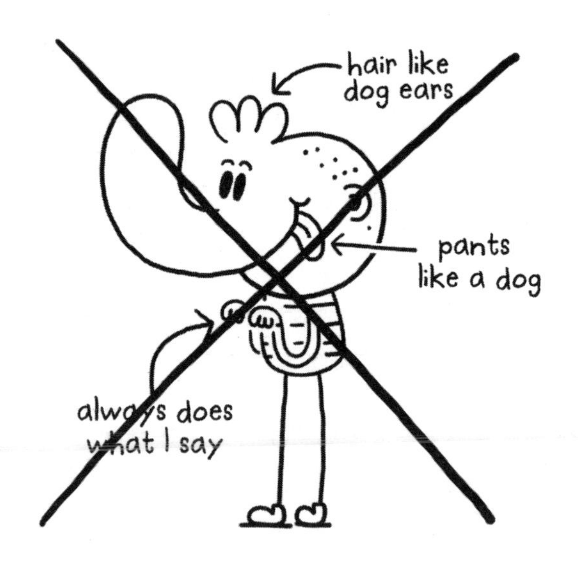

I pointed towards the sea and waggled my hand for Bunky to scamper off. 'Shoo, get out of here!' I shouted, but Bunky just looked at me and smiled.

'What's got into you, Barry?' he said, grinning round at everyone like his ex-owner had gone comperleeterly mad.

I stared at Bunky's stupid scratch-and-sniff Diplodocus sticker, then down at the kitten book in his hands.

'This!' I said, grabbing it and throwing it on to the ground. The only problem was, I'd gone back to being rubbish at throwing again.

The book fluttered through the air like a ginormerous pink moth, towards the wooden cut-out of Gino.

'Wooden Cut-Out Gino! Watch out!' I shouted, as it crashed into his nose and snapped it off.

Real-life Gino stood up and his chair fell over. He waddled over to the window and put his hand over his mouth, staring down at his snapped-off wooden nose.

'Barry, what have you done?!' screamed my mum, running over to Gino. 'Gino, are you all right? I'm so sorry, this isn't like Barry at all!' she said.

Gino looked down at his nose, then up at me, and he shook his head. 'I'm afraid I think it is, Mrs Loser,' he said.

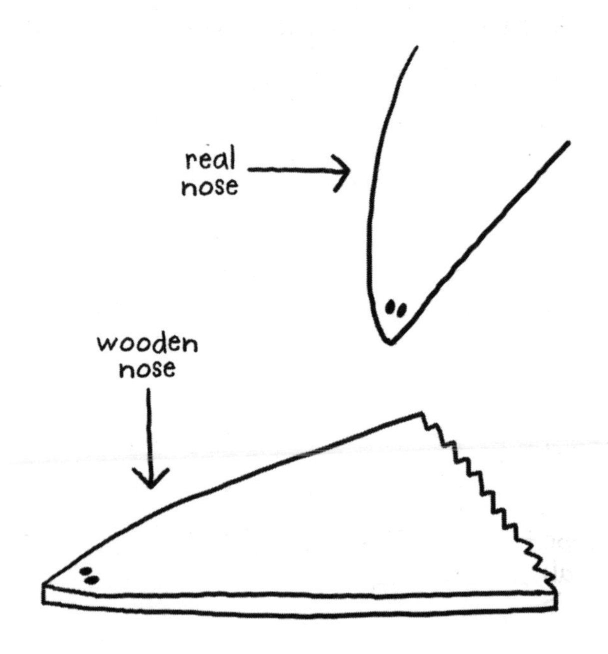

Cabbage puppy

'I hope you're happy with yourself,' said my mum three hours later, once she'd finished shouting at me. Then she slammed the bedroom door.

'Oh yeah, I'm really happy with myself being stuck in a caravan with HIM!' I roared, pointing at Bunky, who was lying on the bottom bunk, holding Nancy's bent-in-half kitten book.

Nancy looked at me from her mattress like she didn't know who I was any more.

'I-I'm sorry about your book,' I mumbled, and I opened the door and trudged towards the kitchen table.

My mum and dad were tucked up in their bedroom and Sharonella and her granny were outside in the yellow tent, keeping all the badgers awake with their snoring.

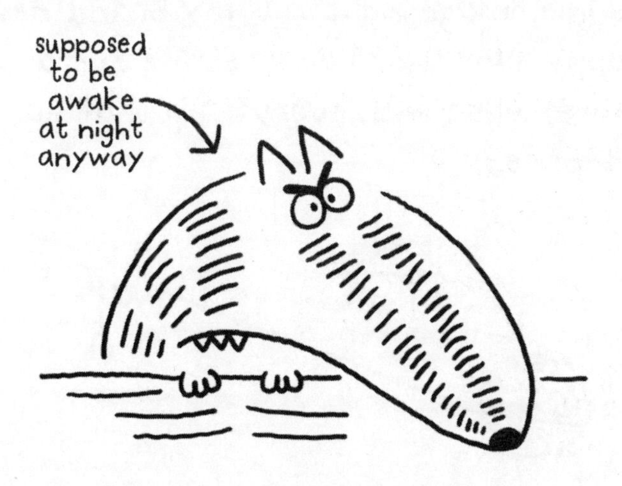

A cabbage sat on the table, ready to be boiled for tomorrow's lunch, and I remembered my dad leaning his head on my mum's tea-towel shoulder, asking if I wanted to invite my friends to Plonkton.

'Some holiday of a lifetime this turned out to be!' I laughed, even though I wasn't in a laughing sort of mood.

I picked the cabbage up and gave it a cuddle, imagining it was my brand-new puppy. Not that I was getting one any more, what with everything that had happened.

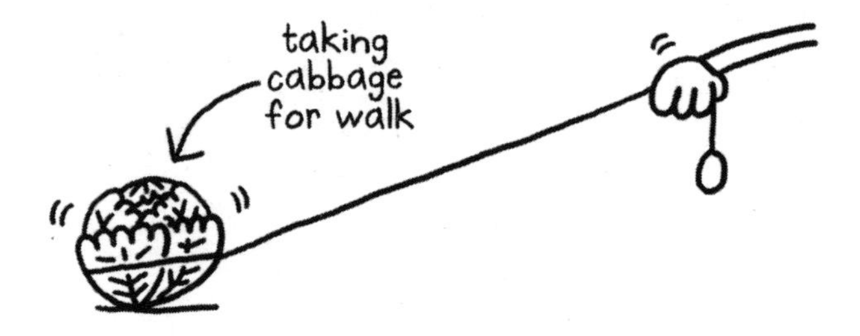

I thought of Gino, opening his caravan door and getting stinksplatted in the face, then I pictured Bunky and Nancy, strolling along Plonkton pier with their stupid arms around each other's shoulders.

I curled up underneath the kitchen table and grabbed a blanket off the chair. 'Goodnight Plonkton,' I said, dozing off to sleep in the banana moonlight.

Worst holiday ever

It was the next morning, and I was sitting on Plonkton beach all on my own, even though I wasn't supposed to leave the caravan.

I'd sneaked out before anyone was awake and walked down the path in the drizzle, trying to come up with one of my brilliant and amazekeel plans to make Gino feel better.

'Worst holiday ever,' I wrote in the sand with my finger, and I waited for a wave to wash the words away.

'Worst holiday ever,' read an annoying voice from behind me, but I didn't even bother turning my head.

'Mornkeels, Shazza,' I said.

She scuffed her shoe on the sand and cleared her throat. 'Er, there's someone here wants to talk to you, Bazza,' she said, and I rolled my head round and counted six feet.

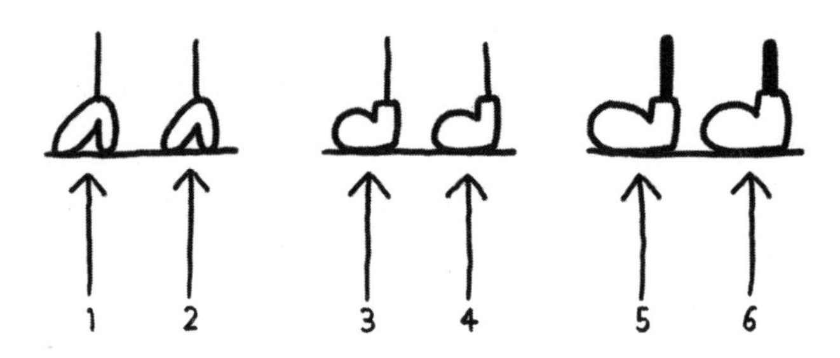

Nancy and Sharonella pushed Bunky forwards and he smiled down at me, but not as much as he would have if I was Nancy. 'Sorry for saying Gino's was all dusty and falling apart,' he said.

I stood up and got on my tiptoes, staring into Bunky's eyes. 'You think this is all about Gino's?' I said. I couldn't believe my ears, eyes, mouth, nose, legs and tiptoes all put together.

'Er, yeah?' said Bunky, scratching his bum, and a tiny little plane started flying over.

'THIS ISN'T JUST ABOUT GINO'S, YOU STUPID DOG!' I shouted over the plane noise, and I remembered that afternoon outside Feeko's when I first realised Bunky fancied Nancy.

'What is it about then, Barry? Is it because you haven't got a scratch-and-sniff sticker?' said Nancy.

'Because if it is, you can have mine,' she smiled, and she started peeling her mushroom one off her dress.

'Thanks Nancy, but it isn't that either,' I said, even though I did still really really want a scratch-and-sniff sticker.

'Thing is . . .' I mumbled. 'You see . . .'

'WHAT?!' shouted Nancy.

'OH, IT'S THIS WHOLE LOSEROIDISH LOVE THING!' I blurted, picking a pebble up and throwing it into the sea.

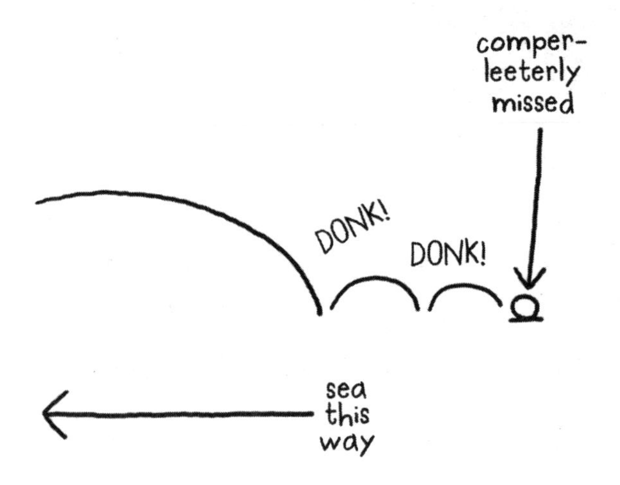

'I spose I just don't like my sort-of pet dog and sort-of pet cat being boyfriend and girlfriend,' I said.

And that's when Nancy started cracking up.

Bunky's but

'Boyfriend and girlfriend?' screamed Nancy. 'Me and Bunky, boyfriend and girlfriend?!' she laughed, folding over in half and dropping to her knees, pounding the sand with her hands.

I looked at Bunky and watched his face turn the same colour as that Feeko's bikini, except less frilly.

'W-we're not?' he stuttered. 'I-I mean, you don't . . .'

'Oh, Bunks!' said Sharonella, putting her arm round him, and Bunky's bottom lip started to wobble.

'But . . .' he said, and his but floated off in the wind. 'Wahhh!' he screamed, running after it, and I watched him turn into a dot.

Crabby Wabby

'Bunky!' I shouted, scrabbling over the rocks with Nancy and Sharonella. Maybe it was seeing his face go pink and almost start to cry, or maybe it was finding out that Nancy didn't fancy him. All I knew was, I suddenly wasn't annoyed with my sort-of pet dog any more.

'Go away!' he snarled when we found him, curled up on the sand next to a tiny see-through crab. 'At least my Crabby Wabby loves me,' he said, picking up a bit of old ice cream cone someone had dropped and offering it to the crab.

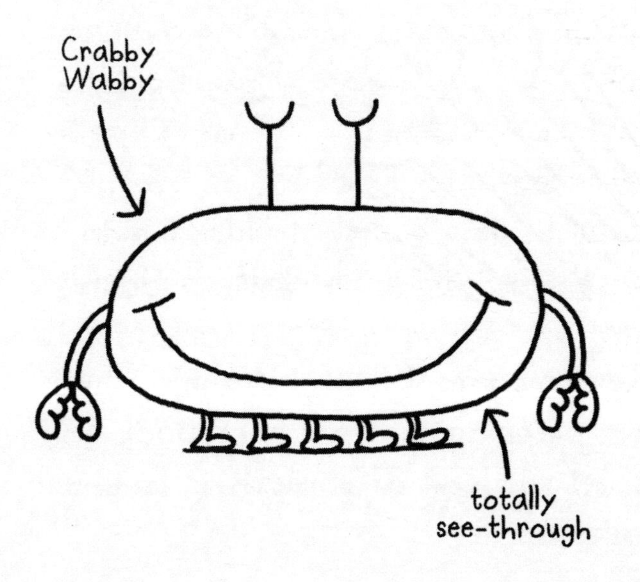

The crab took a sniff of the cone and pincered Bunky's finger with its claw. 'ARGGHH!' screamed Bunky, waggling his hand around. 'Get this stupid thing off me!' he wailed, as I grabbed his arm and Nancy cupped her hands around the crab.

'There you go, Crabby Wabby,' she said, plopping it into a rock pool, and I tried to think of something to cheer Bunky up.

I stuck my hand in my pocket and scrabbled my fingers about, pulling out an ancient old dusty Thumb Sweet. 'Here doggy,' I said, throwing it at his head, and as he opened his mouth to eat it, his eyes spotted something up in the sky.

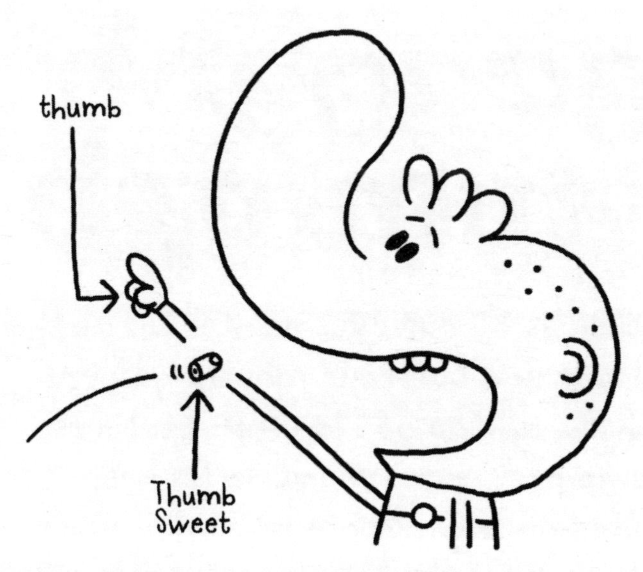

'SEAGULL!' he screamed, and the Thumb Sweet fell down the hole in the middle of his face.

Urrghh
bleurghh
gaagghh
ommmph

All eight of our eyes pointed up at the clouds and our four mouths gasped. There, on top of Plonkton's tallerest lamp post, sat a seagull in his nest. And hanging off the edge of it were Nancy's glasses.

'How we gonna get 'em down?' squawked Sharonella.

You know when you've just swallowed a whole Thumb Sweet and you're pointing your head up so that your neck is bent, and the Thumb Sweet gets stuck in your throat? That's what was happening to Bunky right now.

'Urrghh!' he coughed. 'Bleurghh! Gaagghh! Ommmph!'

Sharonella stopped staring at the seagull and pointed to Bunky. 'I think your dog's choking, Bazza,' she shrieked.

Nancy yelped and scuttled behind Bunky and reached her arms around his belly, giving it a squeeze.

'OOOF!' he blurted, and the Thumb Sweet shot out of his mouth.

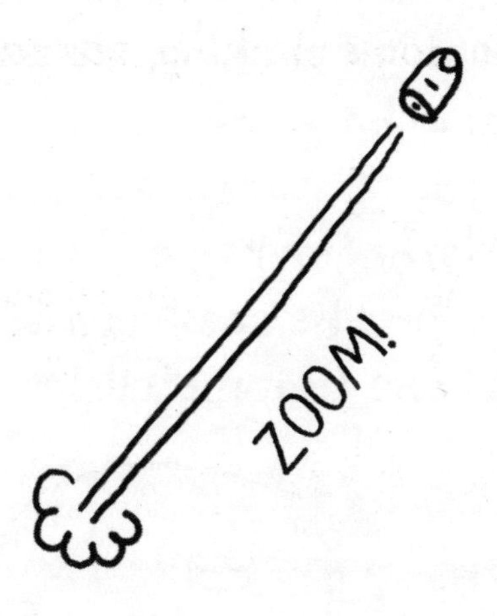

'Look at it go!' I screamed, as it flew into the sky. The seagull's eyes zoomed in on the Thumb Sweet and it swooped out of its nest, making the whole lamp post shake.

'You saved my life, Nancy Wancy!' smiled Bunky, as the glasses wobbled on the edge of the nest.

Up on the seafront road, that old grandad from the day before was driving along in his granny-mobile. 'What you kids all staring at?' he croaked, following our eyes up to the seagull's nest, and he crashed into the lamp post at one centimetre per hour.

The lamp post swayed and Nancy's glasses jerked off the nest, falling through the air like an invisible superhero who wears glasses.

SPLASH! They landed in a rock pool, and Nancy sprinted over.

She lifted her specs out of the water and took Mrs Gino's granny ones off her nose. 'Any time, Bunky Wunky!' she smiled, passing them to me, and I put them on and everyone laughed, including the old grandad.

Once we'd all stopped laughing

'So everyone's back to being friends?' said Nancy, once we'd all stopped laughing. Not that we'd been laughing for THAT long, because me wearing Mrs Gino's glasses isn't THAT funny. (Is really.)

I smiled at Bunky, and he smiled back, just as much as he would if he'd been smiling at Nancy, then I suddenly started to feel a bit queasy, probably because Mrs Gino's glasses were making my eyes go all blurry.

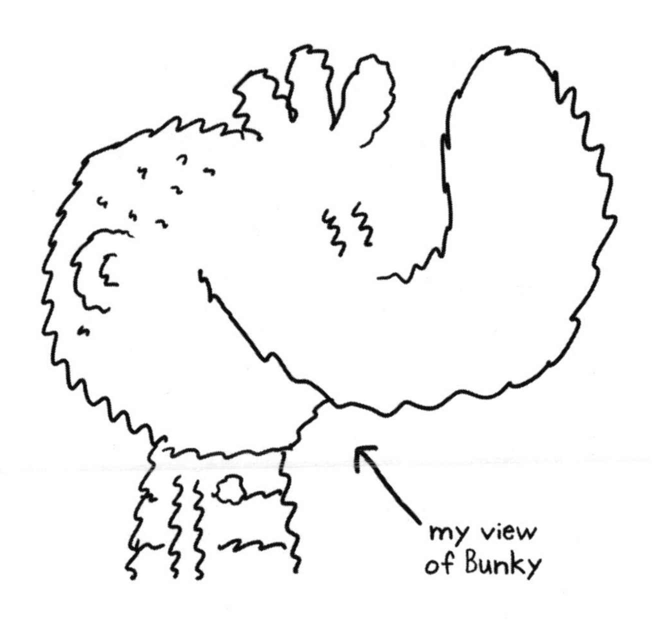

'Poor Gino, if only I could come up with one of my brilliant and amazekeel plans to make it up to him,' I mumbled, and that's when the massive cloud that'd been covering the sun for the whole of our holiday in Plonkton floated two millimetres to the right.

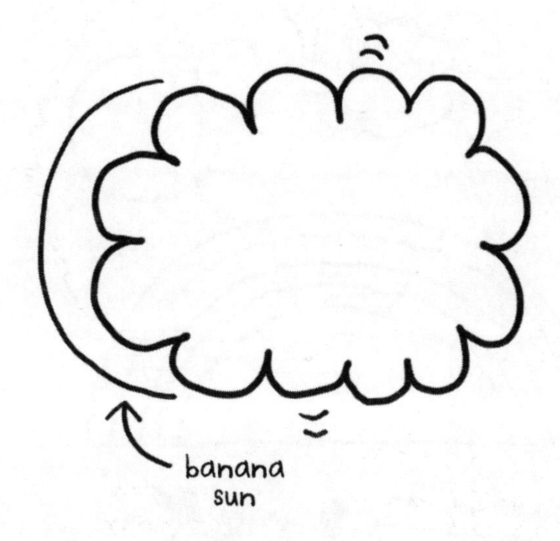

A rainbow shot across the sky, and Bunky's face lit up. He looked down at his pink-paint-covered jumper and smiled.

'Follow me!' he shouted, running off towards the caravans. 'I think I might know just the thing!'

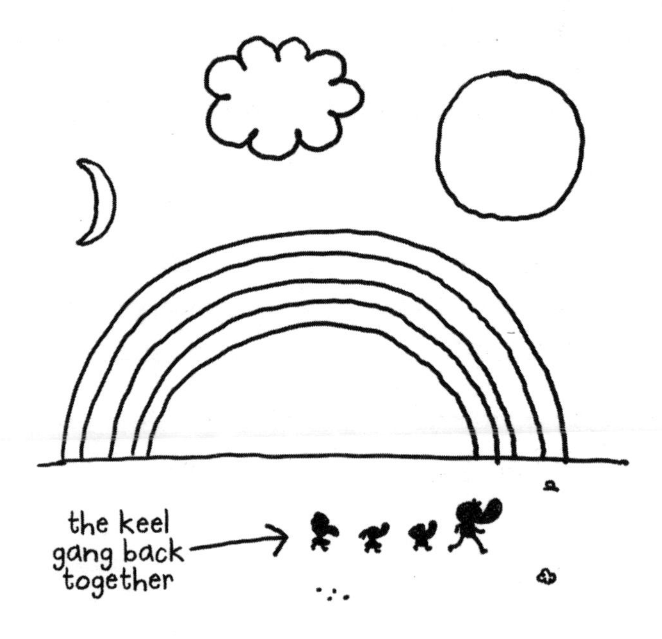

Best holiday ever

It was ten hours, sixteen minutes and twenty-seven seconds later, and I was taking the deeperest breath of my whole entire life on earth amen.

'Welcome to the grand reopening of Gino's Pizza!' I boomed, as the door swung open and everyone in the whole of Plonkton started pouring in.

I smiled at Bunky and he patted me on the shoulder, patting himself on HIS shoulder at the same time. 'How keel was my plan!' he grinned, and I looked around at the All New Gino's Pizza.

'It was brilliant and amazekeel!' said Mr Whatsitcalled, walking past the mended wooden cut-out of Gino and picking up a menu.

'Thanks for letting us use your paints, Mr . . .' I said, and we all twizzled our eyes around.

The walls had been painted like a rainbow, and we'd decorated the tables with keel old Fronkle bottles filled with fake plastic sunflowers.

The floor was shining, thanks to me scrubbing it clean with my mum's washing-up liquid, and the photo of Gino and his wife outside their house had a brand-new frame.

Even the wobbly three-legged chair had four legs now. Although I wouldn't sit on it if you ever go to Gino's, seeing as one of them is made out of a twig.

'I'm so proud of you, Snookyflumps!' said my mum, sitting down in a booth with my dad, who had a tear rolling down his cheek because Banana Moon was playing through the speakers.

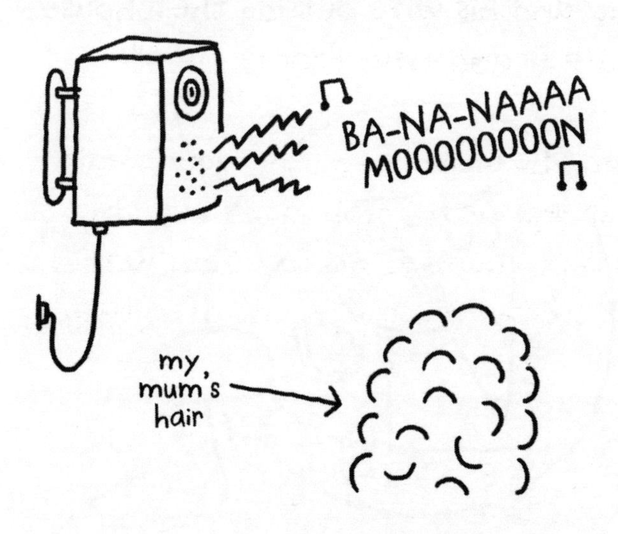

'Twenty plates of Cat Ears coming up!' crackled an excited old voice from the kitchen, and I spotted Gino with Sharonella's granny, who'd offered to help, what with how busy Gino's was.

Gino peered through his glasses and gave me a thumbs up, and I thought back to a week ago, when all I ever wanted was one of Miss Spivak's scratch-and-sniff stickers.

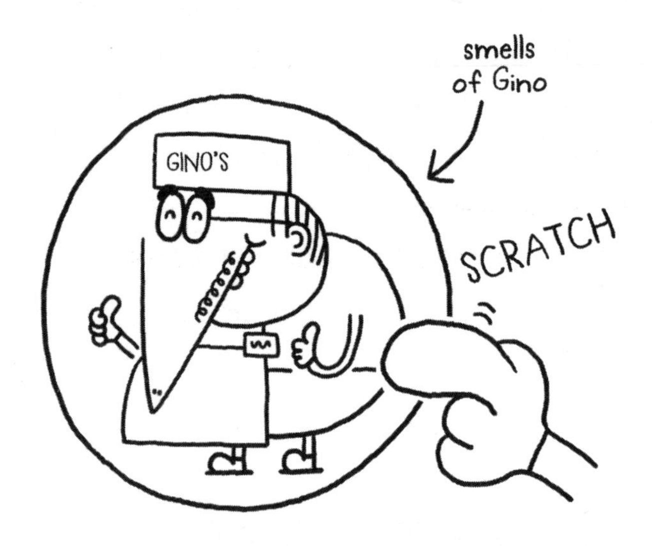

'Who needs them!' I smiled, scratching my bin-smelling 23p price tag, and I spotted Trev or Trevor walking in with Threelegs.

Threelegs was dragging his bum across the floor, right in front of where Nancy and Sharonella were stuffing Cat Ears into their mouths.

'Come on Bunky,' I said, squidging in next to Sharonella, and he shuffled his bum along until he was opposite me. I reached my hand out for a high-five, and the noise of all four of our palms slapping together made me blink.

When I opened my eyes again thirteen billiseconds later, my mum was standing next to our booth, smiling like it was Christmas morning. 'What is it?' I said, even though I didn't need anything else. I had my half-dog, half-best-friend back and everything was keel times a millikeel.

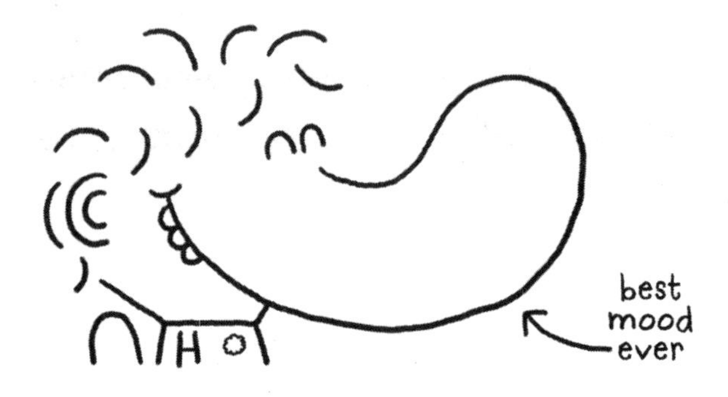

'Now Barry, I know how upset you were about not getting a puppy,' said my mum, taking a bite of her Cat Ear with extra cucumbers on top. 'And you've been SUCH a good boy, helping Gino out like this . . .'

'Ye-ah?' I said, splitting my yeah into two bits because of how much I was wondering what she was going to say.

'Well, you know how I've been going on about babies quite a lot recently?' she said, and I nodded. She put her hands on her tummy and gave it a squeeze. 'Forget about boring old puppies, Barry Warry!' she smiled. 'I'm having another Snookyflumps!'

My dad leaned his head on her shoulder, waggling his cabbagey eyebrows. 'If it's a boy I thought we could call him Frankie Teacup!' he chuckled, and the words swam down my earholes, exploding in my brain like the ginormerest stinksplat ever.

'NOOOO!!!' I screamed, running out of Gino's Pizza and down towards the beach, until all you could see of me was a tiny little dot.

But that's a comperleeterly different story.

THE END!

Or is it?

Yes.

(Until the next one.)

About the chooser of the colour of the cover

Jim Smith is the keelest kids' book colour-of-cover-chooser in the whole world amen.

He graduated from art school with first class honours (the best you can get) and went on to create the branding for a sweet little chain of coffee shops.

He also designs cards and gifts under the name Waldo Pancake.

'I've been choosing cover colours for a while now. This is my fifth book!' says Jim, holding up a selection of differently coloured book covers like he's in an advert or something.

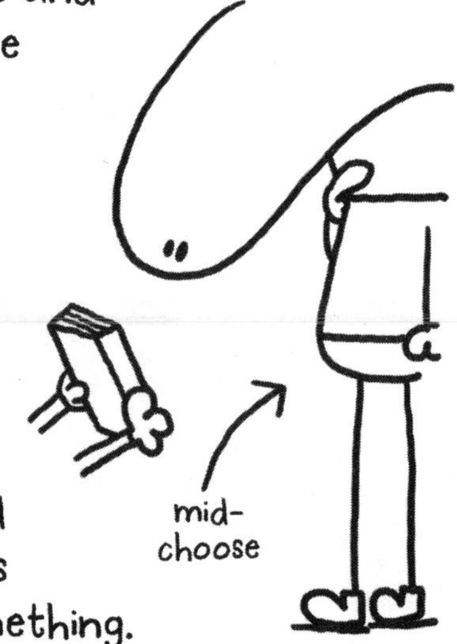